LICA

House of Frazier Book 1

KATHI S. BARTON

World Castle Publishing, LLC
Pensacola, Florida
Copyright © 2024 Kathi S. Barton
Paperback ISBN: 9798891261723
eBook ISBN: 9798891261730
First Edition World Castle Publishing, LLC, March 11, 2024
http://www.worldcastlepublishing.com

Licensing Notes

Cover: Cover Designs by Karen
Cover-designs-by-karen.com
Editor: Karen Fuller

Chapter 1

"Run." When they only stood there staring at him, Lica finally shoved his two brothers in the direction of the woods to get them going. If they were caught by their father, he'd knock them out and then blame the accident that he'd caused on them. As they were getting away, it was Edmond, his brother closer to his age, who shifted — which is something they rarely did, especially out in the open like they were, but he was getting further away with each bound of his paws. When Guy, another younger brother, did the same, Lica hoped they would be far enough away that no one noticed. Christ, he hoped so. That's all they needed was for their father to know that they could shift into a wolf after all this time when they'd been hiding it from their parents since birth.

Since their mother was a wolf, not even a full-blooded one, and their father was a human, the chances of them being able to shift were slim. The six of them, since they were old enough to be able to shift at ten, had been told to keep it from their parents or they'd use their ability not just against them but other people as well. It had been easy for them to hide it, so far anyway, since their mother couldn't shift either. Lica thought it was the only thing that had saved their lives a lot during their childhood so far. Being able to shift to heal their wounds after a severe beating from them.

"Where are they? Them other two? Where'd they go?" Knowing that he was testing his father's already short temper, he asked him who he meant. The slap to his face knocked him backward, rolling him down the hill enough that he'd not be able to get to him quickly. Lica laid there. "Your fucking brothers. Where did they go? One of you is gonna take the blame for this, and I'm guessing it might well be you. You fucking shit."

He didn't mind the name calling. In fact, Lica rarely noticed him being called anything but some version of *fucking* something his entire life.

There were other names that he was called, rarely Lica Frazier, which was his real name. None of his brothers were ever called by their given name.

Climbing up the hill when the police arrived, he stayed as far from his father as he could. Mother hadn't been with them this time, which was a good thing. She would have surely noticed that the other two could shift. And that, as they say, would have been the literal end of all six of them. The three with their father, and the three at home with their mother.

"Damned boy, there was driving." He'd not been, and he was positive that the officer knew it. Dan Wilkins. At sixteen, Lica could pass for a person ten years older, but Dan knew how old each of them was since he'd been around when they'd been born. He was a part of their wolf pack. "Trying to get him to stay on the straight and narrow is damned near impossible with them other ones screaming in the back seat."

Dan spit out his tobacco juice before speaking. "Don't see no other kids, Fred. You been drinking again?" Dan leaned in and sniffed father. "Yeah, I'll say you've been drinking a great deal. And that boy there, he wasn't driving. I told you last month we got us some camera's all over the place now, just about on all the roads. I saw you getting out of the driver's door."

"You calling me a liar, Daniel?" Dan said that he was on account of him lying to him again. "I don't know what you're talking about. That boy there, he was driving and the one that tore out Mr. Charles's fencing when he swerved off the road." Father laughed. "It don't matter to me, none who you think was driving. That little fucker is the one that is going to be putting the fence back up for knocking it down. And you call me a liar again, and I'll snap your head off where your mouth is."

"You're not above the law, Fred Frazier. You best be remembering that. Now, I'm going to ask you again, you driving that car? Remember what I said? I got us cameras all over the place now." Father glared at him, but Lica knew he'd not hit him in front of the police. For all his blustering, his father was afraid of the police more than he was their mother. And she was terrifying to every living soul in the world. They all knew that.

"I was driving. But I ain't going to be putting that fence back up. That's what I got these damned kids for. Doing the work that I don't want to." Officer Wilkins said he'd see about that, and Lica knew that their father would be putting up the broken fence, and they'd be getting the beaten for him having to do it.

Officer Wilkins told him to get under the wheel to drive the car back to his home. That it was all right this time. Father was put in the back of the cruiser and locked in before Lica was ready to admit that he was terrified. Hanging onto the handle of the driver's side door, he counted to twenty, four times, just to keep himself from falling over before he turned and talked to the officer.

"You gonna get your ass beat, ain't you, boy? You tell me the truth now. You hear me?" He said yes, sir, that they all would. He wasn't going to lie to him anyway, the man carried a gun, and that was for sure more dangerous than his drunk father was right now. "Your brothers, they out there someplace? Hiding?"

"Yes, sir. I didn't know what he'd do to them when you showed up. So I sent them on their way." Lica glanced at the cruiser with his father sitting in the back. "He ain't going to like you talking to me like this either. He's going to think I'm telling you falsehoods."

"I'll tell him you didn't say a word. Won't matter, I don't think, but I'll tell him that." Dan spit again, then looked at him. "I want you boys to come over to my house tomorrow after you've been put to bed. You can do that, can't you? I've seen you out and about working."

"Yes, sir. So long as he's not up and around." He said he'd not be doing much but sleeping when he got home until the fence was up. "We'll be there. Around midnight?"

"Yeah, that sounds about right. I got me some work for you six that will give you some pocket money. I hear tell that your parents aren't paying your dues for school. I'll pay you enough to take care of that and get you some boots, too. I hate to say this to you, but you'll have to find a good hiding place for them so he doesn't find them. He'll sell them off for sure, knowing him." Lica said he had the perfect place. "I'm right sorry that you and the others have to put up with them as your parents. You're good boys, and I hate that he beats on you so much. Both of them do it, don't they?"

"Yes, sir. They're powerful mean when they think we've done something wrong." Dan nodded.

Then he asked him when he'd be eighteen. "I'll be eighteen in thirteen months and three days. But I won't be running unless he makes me. Us brothers, we made us a promise that we'd stay together until we can all leave. And Devlin, he'll be eighteen in four years."

"Gonna be hard, you know that, don't you?" He said that he'd not leave his family behind. "All right then. I'll keep an eye out for you boys. Them fates, they surely did mess up a bit by putting them two together and then giving you boys to them monsters."

He didn't bother agreeing or disagreeing with the man. Dan had known his parents since they were kids together. And from what his grannie had told them when she could visit, was that their father had been just what Dan called him. A monster. So had been their mother.

Driving the car back to the house, he was inside and in his room before his mother noticed him. Checking on the other two, just making sure they made it home, he was glad to see that not only did they make it, but they didn't seem to have been hurt any either.

Their mother would be making her way to

the police station tomorrow. Walking too. None of them had a driver's license but their father. He told them they couldn't have one until he was sure they'd not run off. But they would, licenses or not. Just as soon as they were all of legal age to do it. Just a little over four more years, and they'd be out of here. Lica only hoped that the six of them lived that long.

Over the next month, the six of them chopped wood for Mr. Wilkins and anyone else who had the money to pay them for work. It was hard work, chopping in the dark, but they were able to get plenty done in that time and also were able to put a new roof on Mr. Chance's house, round up Ms. Lane's pigs that got out, and to pick corn and pumpkins for Mr. Brown.

The four hundred dollars they managed to make that was left over from paying their school fees was held onto by Mrs. Wilkins. She even put it all in the bank for them so that they could get it when they wanted. A plan was worked out, too, such that if any of them had some extra cash to put up, they only had to leave it on the back porch under her basket of apples, and she'd put it in the bank. Extra or not, it was going to go into the bank for them to run with. Even if it was ten cents they found on the way into town, it would go into the basket money and be put into the bank.

Over the next several months, the six of them managed to save up just over a thousand dollars. That was after they each got a much-needed pair of boots, coats that they could wear to school, and some paper and pencils for classes. They were all aware that it wasn't a great deal of money. But it was a start, they thought. They didn't take much in the way of chances with the cash, never having it on them when they were at home or working. As soon as they got paid, one of them would go right to the Wilkins home and put it under the basket. It was the only way that they felt safe with having a job. Then, their mother caught them working one night.

He hadn't any idea how she'd figured out that they weren't home that night. She and father had gone to the bar to play cards and get drunk, and that usually meant that they'd be gone well into the afternoon the next day. They'd be too drunk to drive home, so they'd pull into some lot, pull out their tent, and sleep off their drunkenness. It was their Friday night thing to do.

They had been coming back from working at six in the morning, dirty and exhausted, when she found them along the side of the road walking home. Luckily, he supposed they'd left their tools, an axe, and a limb saw at the place they'd been working. Otherwise, Lica was sure that she would have used it on them. Father was out cold, but she was raging mad.

It was the first time that he'd gotten beaten so badly that he had three ribs broken as well as his left arm. The others, Devlin, had a broken collar and enough cuts to warrant him getting fifty or so stitches. But it was Edmond that had gotten the worst of it. Not only did he have broken ribs, nine of them, but he had both arms broken and his left big toe removed when she used her high heel on his foot to club him, she called it.

She was arrested then. Officer Dan had made it out that they were working out some kind of trouble they'd caused and had to be healthy to do it. Unless she wanted to work for their trouble. Which needless to say, she didn't. There wasn't any trouble they caused, of course. But it worked, and Mother ended up in jail. Long enough for them to have healed like humans because shifting would have been dangerous for them.

For the next three months, they were on their own convalescing. If they dared to shift, they'd be all right, but their parents didn't know they could, so none of them risked trying it. He was nearly eighteen by then and was old enough to be able to care for them on his own if it came to that.

Father wouldn't leave the jail because *his love* was there, so they did as much as they could in gathering up food stuffs, and cash while he was gone. It was the most difficult three months of his life. It was a few months later, the day he turned eighteen, that everything went to hell. And the only time in his life when he could honestly say that he hated people. And he hated his parents with a passion that stayed with him for most of his life.

Temptation was nothing he'd ever been swayed by. Not a pretty woman. Not a *too good to be truth* scam, nor was he ever swayed by fast money. All of them had learned the hard way that if their parents were on board with something, it was going to mean jail time for somebody. None of them ever participated in anything that their parents thought up. In fact, they would let the police know about their scams so that if they were caught with them and made to go on their scams for some reason, they wouldn't be a part of the arrests. And there were plenty of arrests for their parents the older they got, until his birthday.

~*~

Fred hated his kids. He didn't much care for his wife either, but she was an easy lay, and that's mostly all he wanted from her. Paula hated their kids too, mostly Lica, but she would beat them until they were bloodied every time she got the chance. Fred didn't feel sorry for his boys. Hating them with a passion took care of that. But he decided one afternoon that if he was able to get rid of the oldest one, the others would fall in line with what he wanted more often than they did now. Mother fuckers weren't even good for scaring people with their beasts. None of them had one.

"You'd think that with having six kids that, one of them would be a wolf like you are, wouldn't you, Paula?" She told him that she wasn't a pureblood either, so it didn't stand to reason their kids would be. Then she reminded him, as she did every time, that she couldn't be a beast either. "Yeah, I know you can't shift, Paula. You don't need to tell me every time I say something about it. But one of them should have been, don't you think? I mean, your sister, she has her nine kids, and all of them are wolves. I probably should have married her. That would have been better suited to me in getting some scary kids."

"If you'd of married up with my sister there wouldn't have been nothing for you to use to father them boys. I would have cut you to the wick. You can bet your ass on that." She turned and looked at him. "What are you thinking about Tally for? She's worse off than we are with feeding her kids. At least ours don't come to the table all the time expecting something for them to eat. We trained them good in not expecting anything from us."

"Yeah, that's true, that's true." He smiled when he saw his boys out in the yard. They were just sitting there under the tree that they had them chained up to, not saying a word. "I'm thinking that the next time we have to discipline them, we should kill them off. Ain't no law against us killing them if they've been horrible kids, is there?"

"You don't remember all that trouble I got into when I beat them for working? I still don't believe for a minute that they were only working for food. But nobody would tell us if they were getting paid real money. And I hate that them people tried to shame us by saying we should have fed them better than we did. Fuck that shit. If I had to feed them every time they were hungry, I'd not have time to have myself some relaxing time." She turned and looked at him again. "What are you thinking about by killing them off?"

"How old is Lica now? I'm betting he's an adult. We should make him work at a real job someplace. I don't know why all of them ain't working at a real job bringing us home some cash." She said that it would mess up their food card. "Not if nobody knows about it, it won't. Besides, if any of them is eighteen or better, we won't be getting food money for them anyway. We already had them tested for being stupid. They said that they're all smart boys but not wolves."

That bothered him to this day that his boys were just plain old humans like he was. The only reason that he agreed to be married to Paula was her being a wolf and her daddy being the alpha. Then, not ten days after they'd been married, Lica senior had went and picked a fight with a young pup and lost not just his life and his pack but all his land and money, too. Fred was thrilled beyond words that he and Paula had been on their honeymoon then, or they would have been killed too. Just like the entire pack had been. Damn, but it was a wholly mess.

The only person that had managed to get away was his momma. He still didn't know how that had come to be. But she'd been helpful to them for a few years. Her being a doctor of their kind and having a full-time job that paid them real well and kept them in nice things. Then she up and thought that she'd not be helping them anymore. She told him that she didn't like the way that they treated her grandsons. Stupid woman. There was no threatening her either to make her stay. One day, they got up, and she was gone. Couldn't find her either. Damned woman. All women were stupid as far as he was concerned. But he didn't say that very loud when his wife was around. She'd kill him off for sure if he did.

They had to hide out for weeks after the pack was taken over. Them just being married and just being the two of them made it a sight better at hiding than it would have nowadays and all so that the pup and his crew didn't find them. He didn't know anything about that kind of thing going on when he arranged to marry Paula. And he wouldn't have if he'd known that was possible if someone else came along to take over the pack. They joined them a new pack, and then his mom came for a bit to stay with them after the boys started popping out like them Pez candies.

"What are you mumbling about?" Fred nearly told his wife it was none of her business, but he caught himself just in time. "I looked it up, Fred. Today is Lica's birthday. Imagine that. It's today like you planned it. What did you have planned for him to be gone from here? I, for one, would like to have them all disappear, but that one, well, you know how much I hate him."

"I've been thinking that he's going to get into a tussle with the cops. You and me, we'll knock ourselves up a bit, then call the cops. He won't know a thing about it until they kill him dead. We don't have to be drawing too much blood, but enough for them to take him away. And if that one works, we'll get the rest of them arrested, too. Whatcha think about that?" She told him she didn't want to be too knocked around. "No. I'll hit you once, and you can hit me one time. After that, we'll lay low until he comes in tonight — did they say where they were going when we chained them up this morning?"

"No, they didn't say shit. I know that they're not out there keeping their mouths shut under the tree like we told them, so whatever they doing, they're not doing anything to bring in any money, you can bet that for sure." Yes, he knew that for sure. They were lazy fuckers, the lot of them. "All right. I like that idea. We'll get it going tonight, and then we'll rid ourselves of them kids for good."

Fred wished he'd been the first one to hit. He knew that Paula was gonna knock his head off for sure. He could tell by the way that she was tensing up that she was gonna hammer his head, but good. Closing his eyes, ready for whatever hit him, he heard the front door open up and turned to look to see if it was one of their kids coming in. It wasn't his kids but some man he thought that he should be knowing.

"What do you want?" Fred looked at his wife and then at the man standing in the doorway. He didn't have any idea who he might be, but apparently Paula knew who he was. "You get on out of here. I told you already that we don't pay dues on account of us not wanting to be a part of your pack. Go on now. You're interrupting our business."

"I told you two months ago, Paula that I was going to be giving you a deadline to be paying your dues. You've been a part of my pack, whether you want to be or not, for the last nineteen years. It's totaled up to be a nice sum of money. And the pack needs it. Pay up, or I'm going to have to take something from you." Fred asked him what he was talking about. "I'm your alpha, Lincoln Bates, you deadbeats. Yearly dues is what I'm talking about. You and your family came here to be a part of my pack when you were nothing but newlyweds. I gave you a year's grace in not paying on account of you having to take care of your old momma. Well, she's not been here for decades, and I'm sick of you being in every line there is to be getting free handouts without paying your dues. I told your wife that I was going to be around to collect them and that's what I'm here for. You owe thirty-six hundred dollars in dues and another thirty-six hundred dollars for me having to come here and collect them. Pay up or face the consequences. I'm finished playing with you people."

Fred didn't know how it had happened, but it was a blur of moment, and he fell to the floor. Paula was screaming so loud that it hurt his ears, but he couldn't get her to stop. Moving his mouth was too much work, so he just moaned his unhappiness at her to get her to stop. Closing his eyes against the movements again, he felt himself be sick and turned to his side and puked up his dinner. Damn, but it didn't taste any better the second time than it did the first, either. Paula was one of the worst cooks he'd ever encountered. Not like his momma could cook. She could — When someone said his name, he turned to look.

Fred couldn't get anything to focus in his eyeballs. The man was a big man, bigger than he was anyways, but he didn't know who he was. Looking around the room made him ill again, but he thought that he should know the bunch of men in the room with him and his wife. It was his house, wasn't it? That should count for something, he thought.

"You're dying." He told the man that he wasn't doing any such thing. "You're near dead now. Any last words you'd like to say to Mother? She's gonna live, mores the pity, but you are as good as dead right now."

"Who are you?" He was having trouble working up enough spit to talk, but the man answered him. He said he was his son, Lica. "You were supposed to be blamed for beating us up. I'm going to tell the police that you did it when they get here, too."

"You're not going to be able to tell anyone anything if you don't lay still and stop from bleeding everywhere. As I said, you're dying. You were shot in the chest by Mother. She was aiming for the Alpha, but he moved you in front of the shot." His son, or whoever he was, looked away and then back at him. "Mr. Bates said that he heard what you were planning, and he's going to tell the police on you when they get here. There they are now, pulling into the drive. Mother is going to be going to human prison, too, if she lives. I don't see a reason why she won't live, but you never know about wounds to the belly." He heard his wife screaming again. Then she started jabbering about one of them doing the plan they had.

"You take his place, you mongrel. You hear me? That's the very least you can do for me since I've had to put up with you for the last twenty-some years." He tried to get Paula to come closer to him, but he was getting weaker by the minute. Maybe he was dying. He surely did feel weak. But he could hear his Paula planning as clear as day. "One of you boys, get over here and tell them that you shot your momma. I'm not going to prison. You hear me? Your daddy ain't going to go to prison either when it was you six that we was going to kill off. Come on over here and bring me that cop's gun. I'll shoot the six of you, and that'll be the end of my troubles. Even your daddy shouldn't have to die until I said he can. You hear me?"

Fred could hear her fine but what she was saying was making his head spin a little. Another person was in his vision, and he asked who they were. He said his name was Lincoln Bates and that he was going to have the pack take care of his body when it was released to him. For some reason, Fred didn't think that it was going to be a good thing taking care of him.

He did get to see the police. There seemed to be about fifty of them the way that they kept moving around and such. There was someone laughing, too. He didn't know who that was, but he thought it rude to laugh like that when someone was supposed to be dying. He couldn't remember who was dying, but he did remember someone telling him that someone was.

When he opened his eyes again, he didn't know where he was. There wasn't much to see. Everything was white like the snow and clean. Paula didn't keep a good house, so he knew that he wasn't home anymore. While he'd been lying on the floor one day after Paula hit him, he'd seen dust bunnies about forty inches long. Looking around hurt, so he tried to call out to someone to talk to him. The little squeak that came out of his mouth embarrassed him some, but that was about all he could manage right now.

"Mr. Frazier? You have anything to say about why you were shot?" He asked him where he was. "You're in the emergency department of the hospital, but you're not going to be alive much longer. You've lost a great deal of blood, and the wound is in a serious location, the doctors are saying. Can you tell me your version of what happened tonight? I've already heard from your alpha and wife. Their versions are a bit different from each other's."

Could he? He had no idea. Then he

remembered what his wife said about their kids. He told the officer as best he could what had been planned out. How they were going to blame it on the kids, so they'd be going to prison and away from them.

"We hate them, you know. All they've done is suck us dry. I want them dead. You hand your gun over to my wife, and she'll take care of them for us. I don't want them around." The man asked if he was serious. "As death."

Chapter 2

Lica leaned against the shovel that he'd been using and looked at his brother's truck as he pulled into the yard. Edmond had been out getting feed for the cattle. The empty truck made him think that things hadn't gone as well as he'd hoped they would.

"No credit, I'm assuming." Edmond shook his head and said that they'd hit their limit with the Barn, the only place around here where someone could buy feed for cattle and such. "I guess we'll be turning them out to the other pasture a little sooner than we thought. That sucks, too, since we need it to get them through the winter months."

"I got a call into the Callus farm." Without saying a word, Lica turned his back to his brother and began shoveling the shit out of the stall. "It's a good deal, Lica. All we have to do is run their tractors for them for six months, then it'll be all ours. I've looked over the contract and had Ivan look at it, too. The only loopholes in it are in our favor. At least our cattle will be able to eat for the fall and winter months and right on until spring of next year."

"I don't like having to get things on credit, Edmond. And we both know that's what they mean when they say we'll be paid well." He said he knew that, but they had to eat. "I guess it can't hurt for us to do the work. They still all right with us using their equipment for the south field?"

"Yes. In fact, it was their idea for us to get it ready for winter. You know as well as I do that's going to save us a bunch of trouble. Our tractor isn't going to make it another year, and this one, buying on credit like they said, will get us through a lot of years." Lica knew that, but he didn't have to like it. "I have the contract with me now. It's been signed off on everyone but you. And since you have the most experience in driving the larger equipment, they're going to pay you extra for teaching their hands on how to use it when we get there."

Lica signed his name to the bottom of the contract where all the others had. They'd been partners in their farming since the day that Devlin had turned eighteen. If not for the help of Dan Wilkins, the cop in town, there is no telling what might have happened to the six of them when their mother was put in prison and their father killed. Turning to look at Edmond when he cleared his throat, he asked him what was going on.

"Do you remember what today is?" He didn't think that there was a time in his life that he would ever forget what the date was today. "We have to go there and make sure that she doesn't get out. I don't know why they'd even consider her being let go, but today is the day. I've already lined up the attorney that we're using. With Devlin being in his last year of college, it's helped us a great deal in knowing who we can trust as attorneys. Are you going with me?"

"I am. Are the others?" Edmond told him that Ivan wasn't going to be there on time, but he was going to be there. "He's got his interview today, right?"

"Yes. If he gets that job, we'll be looking at

a better income for us." The six of them worked and pooled their money. They paid the bills for the ranch out of their money, and then whatever was left over, usually not too much, was divided up between the five younger ones of them. Since Lica worked on the ranch full time, he had room and board, so that made him not need as big a cut of the money. "I had a strange phone call this morning. I don't know if I was cut off or the person was, but they were asking about the year that our father died. I didn't get an opportunity to answer them."

"They'll call back or won't. More than likely, someone trying to get us to pay some money to them. I know that I don't have to ask, but I'm gonna just for my own peace of mind, but you have all the receipts from paying off Bates, don't you? I'm glad that we were able to pay the parents' dues. His letting us pay it over time helped us out a great deal, but I don't ever want a big debt like that hanging over my head again. Do you?" Edmond said that he had copies, and so did their attorney. "All right then. Let me finish up this stall and I'll get myself a shower to get going. Are we going together or meeting up there?"

"There." Nodding, Lica finished up his job

and then made his way to the outside shower. It wasn't anything more than a large tub with a hole in it that hug on the side of the house. But when you needed to rinse off the crap from the barn, it was a better way to clean up than dragging all the nastiness into the house to shower. He was headed to the shower, his clothing hanging on the line after his rinse, when the house phone rang.

"Hello, House of Fraizer." He waited on the line to quiet down before he spoke again. He didn't know the voice, so he didn't hang up on whoever it was because it sounded like an elderly woman. Again, he said the name of their house. It was easier than naming off all of them who lived there until the person spoke.

"Which one of you boys is this? I'm thinking Edmond is who I spoke to earlier but I didn't have a good connection." He said he was Lica. "Lica? My goodness, you don't sound a bit like your father, thankfully. I just heard that the old bastard is dead. Can you confirm that for me? I'll need a year and date, honey."

He gave her the date and the time that his death was confirmed. Still, no idea who he was talking to, and knowing that just about everybody in the state knew how his parents had come to be in trouble, he even told the woman the year that his mother had been sentenced too.

"Her hearing is today, correct? Why they'd want that cunt of a woman out of prison is beyond me, but I don't make the rules." Lica couldn't help it. He laughed. "Oh, you have a good sense of humor. I'm so thrilled to know that. I was wondering if you have some room for an old woman to come and stay with you for a little bit. I can still cook a mean pot roast and bake a lemon cake that will make your toes curl."

It took him less than a minute to know who he was talking to. "Grannie Fraizer? Is this you?" She laughed, her voice coming over the phone as lovely as he used to remember it being when he'd been a child. It was as soothing as a brush of her hand over his head when she'd come to see him to bed. "My goodness. If we don't have any room, you can bunk in my bed, and I'll sleep in the barn. It's nice and warm this time of year for that, anyway. When are you coming?"

"Oh, Lica, I can't believe…well, I should believe you'd be this welcoming. I'll be at the courthouse when they call it to order. I got me a few things I'd like to say about that old bitch that'll have her behind bars for the rest of her days. It will. How are you boys doing?" He told her that they were doing as well as can be. "Liar. You're not doing well at all. I didn't know a thing about my son being dead until just a few weeks ago. Now that I do, I can make some things...well, I'll see you boys, all of you men now, I guess, at the court house. My goodness, I just can't wait. I'm all giddy to see you. You tell me who they are now, I won't know them little ones. Why Devlin, he was nothing but a babe when I got out of there."

"He's graduating from college in a few weeks. Going to be the family attorney for us." The back door opened, and he heard Mrs. Wilkins squeal and he covered himself up with his free hand as best he could. "I gotta get me some clothing on, Grannie Frazier. I'll tell the others that you're coming. I'm not sure who will remember you, but I can't wait."

"I'm looking forward to it too, son. You've no idea." After hanging up with his grannie, he told Mrs. Wilkins he was sorry.

"You get yourself dressed. It's my fault. I should have knocked first. In my head, well, not today. You are still boys." She was flittering about the kitchen while he ran up the stairs. When the door opened again, he heard his brother Edmond laughing, so he knew that she'd told him she'd caught him standing in the hall naked. Coming down the stairs, Mrs. Wilkins started talking like they'd been having the same conversion as they'd been having five seconds ago, and it being a week ago. "I put them pies in the freezer for you boys. Now, don't be putting them in the micro-zapper or they'll not be fit to eat. There are some homemade noodles that I made up in batches for you for your supper, too. Just cook them until they float, and they'll be good with anything."

Her husband, Dan Wilkins, had passed away about the time their mother was sentenced to two life terms in prison. No one, not even his doctor, knew that he had cancer, and by the time he was getting his treatments set up, he was gone. It hurt his heart something terrible for Mr. Dan to be gone. But Mrs. Wilkins had made up for them being with their parents.

For some stupid reason that no one could understand, their mother would be coming up for a parole hearing every fifteen years. This was the first one for her. He had it in his mind that the judge had been sweet on their mother and didn't believe a word out of their mouths when they were asked about her and their living arrangements.

The judge did say that he felt sorry for their mother, her being the mother of six sons and was going to lose out on being able to raise them. He must not have been paying attention all that well when they were talking about how much they hated her.

Anyway, the Wilkins' had been there for them since he and his brothers had purchased the Brady Ranch at an auction three months later with a loan from the Wilkins'. Then after Mr. Dan passed, Mrs. Wilkins kept them in food and darned socks since. She was about the best mother they could have had, he thought.

"I just spoke to Grannie Frazier." Edmond remembered her, asking if she was the one that he'd spoken to earlier. "She was. She said she thought that it was you, but she'd had a bad connection."

Edmond made the two of them a sandwich, and Mrs. Wilkins gave them paper plates and chips to go with it. After sitting at the table, he told them what she'd said about coming to visit.

Mrs. Wilkins smiled at them and asked if they remembered she was going to visit her younger daughter next week.

"I did forget. But this couldn't be more perfect timing, could it?" Edmond winked at him. They both knew that their daughter was going to try to convince her mother to live with her from now on. That living on the farm, ten acres in all was too much for the elderly woman. "You're going to have so much fun with your grandkids you're not going to want to come back."

"Oh, I can't wait to hold them. Did I tell you that her oldest is in the school band? Dan would have been so proud of her." She turned away to shed a tear or two, and he and Edmond let her. "Well, I don't know about me staying with her. She'll want me to go shopping and all kinds of things when I get there. I'm a little old for that now."

There was excitement in her voice, and you would have had to be deaf not to have heard it. Over the last couple of weeks, her older daughter, the one that lived nearby them had sold her home and everything in it to go to live near her sister, too, with their mom. Once she was settled in down in

North Carolina with her family, the house up here would be sold to them. Just as Dan had wanted it to be when he passed for a buck. He didn't have any sons to leave it to, and Dan had always treated them like they were his sons. And they treated him and Mrs. Wilkins like their dad and mom. They were that good to them.

The courthouse was packed when they were shown inside. Ivan was there early, saying that the interview went better than he had thought it would. He was hoping to work with the vet in town and then buy out his practice when the older man was ready to retire.

The others, all dressed in their nicest jeans and shirts and ties, were sitting in the row behind the attorney who was hoping to keep their mother in prison for another fifteen years. Lica hoped that they'd dispense with the fifteen-year parole hearings and just throw away the key. When the judge came in, a new one, they all stood up and listened to what was being said.

"My name is the honorable Jane Sabot. I'm here to listen to the two parties today to settle if Mrs. Paula Frazier is eligible for parole or will be imprisoned for—where did this come from? Did

we ever find out?" The bailiff leaned into her ear
and spoke to the judge. She nodded a couple of
times, then rolled her eyes before she thanked him.
"All right. This is the hearing for Paula Frazier to
be eligible for parole after only serving a fifteen-
year sentence of two life terms for killing her
husband, Fred Frazier, and Officer Joey Lipscomb.
Officer Lipscomb succumbed to his wounds
eighteen months after Mrs. Paula Fraizer shot him.
Is there anything else I should know before I have
Paula Fraizer brought in here? By the way, I will
have this room in order no matter what happens
with the offender. I'm to understand that she's
having a hissy fit today and might cause a ruckus.
Anything?"

        Grannie Frazier was let in from the back,
and she walked up to the dais. Once she was there,
she handed over what looked to him like about a
dozen colorful folders and some other items before
she spoke to the judge. When they were finished,
about twenty minutes after Grannie made her way
up there, she came to sit with the six of them. As
much as he wanted to get some hugs from their
Grannie, they were asked to have a seat first.

        "I need me a minute or two to read over

this. I have copies of it already, and so does the attorney for Paula, correct?" The man stood up and nodded like his head wasn't connected as tightly to his shoulders as it should have been. "You have to use your words. I told you this the other day. The woman recording this for us can't make head signs." He said he had the paperwork. "Good. And you've spoken to Mrs. Fraizer, correct?"

"Yes, ma'am, I have. She's none too happy with it, but she is aware of the information." The judge said she didn't care and asked him to have a seat. After about ten minutes, the courtroom was called to order, and their mom was brought out of the back of the room.

"Christ." Lica agreed with his brother Ayden's assessment of the situation. Their mother had aged about fifty years, it looked like. Her hair, usually dyed to a dark red, was as white as Grannie's was but without any style to it whatsoever. Just a stringy mess with a big childlike bow in the back that was as pink as he'd ever seen the color displayed.

Her lips, usually what Grannie called her lip paint whores red, was devoid of any color, and the nothingness bled into her skin so well that it looked like she had no mouth at all when it was closed. She was wearing a prison jumpsuit of blue and green. Two colors that he'd always liked together but never again. It made her look sickly and washed out. Shaking his head, he felt the others sitting in his row sit up straighter when she turned to look at them after being chained to the table that was in front of her.

"There they are. My sons. Never once have they been to see their poor old mother since they made it so that she'd been taken away from them." Mother turned to the judge when she told her to hush. "I'll do nothing of the sort. They killed their daddy like he was nothing to them. Then they go and say that I did the killing so that I'd not see them all grown up. Just look at them there. Acting like I don't mean nothing to them."

"You don't." When Guy stood up after speaking, the rest of them did as well. "A jury of your peers said that you murdered the man who fathered us and another man, too. A police officer who was on duty that day. So, no, you don't mean a thing to us."

No one moved but the six of them standing. Grannie stood up with them, and that set their mother off to cursing up a storm of name calling that had him snicker a little. Her vocabulary had gotten much better at spewing curse words than it did before she left, and he thought it was funny. When the judge, pounding on her desk with a wooden hammer, told them to sit, the six of them sat down as if they'd been pushed. Grannie just stood there staring at their mother without saying a word.

"What are you doing here, bitch? Thinking to keep me in prison, do you? Well, it won't work. I'm getting out and seeing to their deaths like it should have been done all those years ago." The judge had Mother taken out of the room. She was screaming that she had every right to be there, but Grannie just stood there watching. All the while, the judge pounded on her table and asked for order to be made.

Standing up, he put his arm around his Grannie, and she looked at him. She was dazed looking, like for a few seconds there she didn't know where she was or even perhaps who she was. When she put her hand on his cheek, he kissed her fingers and asked her to have a seat. As soon as she did, he did as well. The judge let out a long breath and had mother taken back to the jail.

~*~

Brogan looked at the headstone of her son. Fredrick Allen Fraizer, her only son, had been in his late thirties when he was killed. If she'd known half of what she did now about him, she'd not had any children. Then he'd married that woman, Paula Snow, and he'd become the worst person she'd ever known. Even to her and her late husband had suffered at his hands and that of Paula before her husband died of their abuse, and she got out of there as fast as she could. It was the only way that she could save those boys.

"You were a cruel and mean person, Fredrick. Even from birth, there was nothing redeeming about you. If not for those boys you sired, I'd think that your life was a total waste of what it took to make you." She looked around the pretty cemetery and then back to where he was laid to rest. "They did right by you even though I don't know why they did. I'd of put you nearest to the trash dumb and that would have been the last visiting anyone would have done for you. Not that I think those boys have set foot in here since you took your last breath. No, they'd not come here if for only to make sure you're dead. They'll do the same for their mother, too. Make sure that the witch is gone forever."

The marker for her son was also made for Paula to rest beside him someday. There was nothing much on the marker to mark his passing but the dates of their births and then his death. No fancy script to say their names, just block letters of their first and last name. It didn't even say 'mother' or 'wife' just the dates and their names.

"I've come to talk to you about what your dad and I did for your boys. I wish I could have done so to your face, but I didn't know that you were dead all these years. After I left here long ago, I went to a place that—well, after your dad died, you killing him off, I mean, I had to go and get myself healed from the beatings that you laid upon me. Nearly died myself, thanks to you, but when I heard that you were dead, I did myself a little dance and had a bottle of champagne too. I'll never think of you again after I leave here today, Fredrick. Only to tell them boys what your father and I did in spite of having you around. As I said, you were a cruel and mean man, and I will never forgive you nor that wife of yours for what you did to your father and I."

After spilling her heart of all the things that she wanted to say to her son, she made her way to her daughter's grave. No one knew that she'd birthed her little girl but her husband. And he took his knowledge of her to his grave, as he promised that he would. Laying the dozen white roses on the infant's headstone, she kissed her fingers and laid them upon the small stone that was Lillies. Telling her little girl, who only lived for a few hours, that she loved and missed her, Brogan made her way to her car and sat under the steering wheel to sob out her misery. And that was the worst kind of misery for her, to lose her daughter so close to her being born to them.

On her way home, she stopped at the store and picked up some flowers that she was going to have on the table, as well as a couple of pies for dessert. Brogan had put a huge pot roast on when she'd left this morning and knew by the time the boys got home, the entire house would smell delicious. The potatoes were all ready to go, and there were fresh green beans simmering on the stove, too. Bread, three loaves that she'd made that very morning was ready to put into the oven then she was going to have a meal with her grandsons. The first of many, she hoped.

Changing into her comfy clothing, she heard a knock at the door. Going to the front of the house, she was surprised to see an older man and woman standing there. She knew right away they were wolves, but she didn't mention that when she let them into the house. Whatever they wanted, she'd take care of it for her grandsons.

"Hello, Mrs. Frazier." Brogan told him to call her by her given name. "Thank you for that. I don't suppose the men are home, are they? I've been missing them about daily, and I need to have a word with Lica."

"He's in the barn. Something about breeding going on. I don't know my way around a cattle ranch, but I can cook one of them up if it's given to me." Both the man and woman laughed. "What is it I can do for you? They're not late on dues or anything, are they? I've come to live with them for a spell, and I have some things to talk over with them."

"No. They're never late with anything." The man laughed a little. "I don't know that they've ever been late for work either but they learned the hard way that they need to be where they're supposed to be and to be there on time, too."

"My son taught them that. The hard way, I'm afraid. What is it that you need from Lica? He's a good boy, all of them are. If you've got something to say to them, I'm going to tell you right now that I might not be a wolf, but I'm meaner than a snake when it comes to the six of them."

"Yes, ma'am, I've no doubt that you're very fond of them. So are my wife and I. In fact, I think the town is about as fond of those boys you call them as they are of their own children. I've come to talk to Lica, him being the oldest, about taking over the pack for me. I'm getting too old to manage it, what with having nineteen grandchildren now and I'd like to retire." She didn't doubt that having grandchildren would take up a lot of time, and she was looking forward to that being a problem for her, too, but she told him that the boys were working. Then she invited them to dinner. "You have no idea how much we were hoping for an invite. As soon as my missus and me stepped on the land here, we could smell that dinner. My goodness, it smells like heaven around here. If you don't mind, we'd love to join you and the boys."

"Good. That's good. I think they'll enjoy that as well. But I have a rule. No business at the table. Not that they have any, but no phones either. It's family time and I take that very seriously when I'm around. These boys of mine are all I have left in the world, and I want to spend as much time as I can with them before I join my husband. You are all right with that. Then I'd love to have you sit with us." It was his wife that said she had the same rule at their home. "Good. Then we'll have a nice dinner and have some nice conversations too. But I will tell you this: Lica isn't going to take that job without some convincing on your part. Not that he'd not be good at it, but he would feel that he isn't good enough. And he's not much on liking people either. None of them are, but Lica is especially no good around humans."

"I've noticed that about all of them. While they'll go to pack meetings, they tend to stand alone, and when it's over, they go home. They're not rude to the others, but they don't have much to do with them. I can understand that, I can but I think this might well be the perfect job for him. And it pays well enough to get them out of debt. They have quite a bit of it, I've heard."

"I'm taking care of that." He smiled at her, and she didn't know what to think about that. "You know something?"

"Yes, ma'am. I don't think that they're going to take anything you have to give them because they feel like they don't want to be beholden to anyone. Even if you're family. They're what you might call afraid of owing anyone."

"I'm going to take care of that too." His smile made her smile, too, but she knew something that they didn't. Brogan was strong-willed, and she knew that they'd take what she had for them, or they'd piss her off. "You'll see. I'm nothing like my son and his wife, but I get what I want. Even if I have to go behind their backs to get what I want."

"Good luck with that." Lica came into the house by the back door, and she stayed in the front room. He had a tendency to come into the house after cleaning up in the nude. It had taken her one time to know that, and she wasn't going to let that happen again. "Lica is mad. I can feel it coming off him like water over a mountain. He's not in the best of humor most of the time. Polite, like I said, but right now, his mood is black."

"Do you know why?" He said that he'd met

his mate. "That's wonderful. Right? I mean, no, it can't be bad to meet her, is it?"

"She's human." Those two words had her laughing. She hadn't a clue why she thought it was so funny, but she couldn't stop herself from laughing. "I'd not let him know you think that it's funny, Brogan. He's about as pissed off as I've ever seen him."

"Oh, I don't care right now. He's met her, and that's the world's greatest…well, they'll come together soon enough. I'm excited to be able to be here when they do. Oh my, I'm about as happy as I've ever been in my life. I want to know everything, but I'll let him tell me. Oh, his mate. Yes, this is the best news I've heard in a very long time. Thank you for telling me."

Chapter 3

Brandy knocked on the door and looked around the yard. She didn't know these people, but apparently, everyone in town knew the Frazier's. When a man opened the door, she asked if she had the correct house and said that she was looking for the Frazier home.

"You've got the right house, but if you're selling something, you're not going to have any luck. Nor will you if you're selling something for your school." He cocked his head at her. "Nah, you're not in school anymore. Maybe college, but no high school. Which Frazier are you looking for?"

"Lica. I don't know if I'm saying that right or not, but he was in my store this morning and made one of my employees cry. I don't usually go to people's houses to complain, but I'm…is he here? Mr. Lica Frazier?" She didn't know why she was talking so much, but the way the man was looking at her made her nervous. Not uncomfortable but nervous all the same. "If not, can you point—"

He didn't move anything but his mouth to yell—loudly for Lica. When someone in the back of the house said he was upstairs, she was invited in to have dinner with them. Before she could tell them no, she already had plans, so the man pulled her into the house and neatly closed the door behind her. Brandy didn't know what to say when four of the biggest men she'd ever seen in her life came into the hallway where she was. Then she got a look at the one that had invited her in.

"I'm not here to cause trouble. I just need to talk to Lica for a minute. And I don't want to have dinner. I'm going to be eating with my parents tonight." There she was again, jabbering. Closing her mouth, she bit her lip so she'd not speak again. It didn't work as well as she hoped. "Why don't I go outside and wait on him?"

"You too good to eat with us?" She saw the man as soon as he cleared the stairs. "When someone invites you to dinner, you're supposed to be polite, not rude."

"Lica, behave yourself. She's wanting to talk to you about you making her employee cry." He told the older woman who had admonished him that he'd done no such thing. "Well, she's here to talk to you about it, so someone isn't telling the truth."

"Are you talking about the Rodeo Burger Joint? That was hours ago." She asked the man who had brought her into this madness how he knew it. "You running that place? I used to work there. For a week. That's the nastiest place I've ever been to."

"Ayden, let her tell us why she's here." There were more people in the room than she could handle. There were now seven men and two older women. The older of the two women was smiling at her, but Brandy suddenly couldn't breathe. Backing away from them, she asked for a moment. "You take as long as you want. Guy, set another plate at the table. Ivan, get her a glass of tea. The sweet stuff. Lica? Why are you just standing there? Take her to the dining room before she passes out. My goodness, you act like you've never seen a pretty woman before. Get going, the lot of you."

She found herself with her head between her knees and being told to breathe. She was trying to tell them that she was all right, but every time she lifted her head, she was shoved back down. It wasn't until someone said something about tea that she was allowed to sit up enough to see. Before she was pushed back down, like she knew that Lica was going to do to her, she punched him in the belly.

"I'm not a flipping yo-yo. Will you stop trying to push me into the floor?" She took the tea and smiled at the person who had brought it to her. "Ivan, right? I don't care for sweet tea. Could you please just get me some ice water?"

"Yes, ma'am, miss?" She said her name was Brandy Conner. They all turned to the man holding his belly and the back of her neck.

"Listen to me, not him. I'm telling you that I want water. He's not my keeper." That got them moving again, and a plate was set in front of her. Lica sat down in the chair next to her. "I came here to talk to you about my employee. You made her cry, which I've found out she does every time something doesn't go her way. I want to know what you said that has her threatening to cut your nuts off. I can understand a little of that, having only spent the last few minutes around you, but what happened?"

"Do you have a weak stomach?" She told him she didn't and asked why. "Ayden worked there about a week a couple of years ago."

"Is this history lesson necessary?" He asked her if she was always so rude when she wanted information from someone. "You're right. My apologies. Go one. So which one is Ayden again?" The man raised his hand as he passed the biggest bowl of mashed potatoes she'd ever seen to her. "Thank you. Go on."

After putting a small scoop on her plate, Lica took the bowl next. After putting about three heaping scoops on his own plate, he put another one on hers. Before she could tell him that she had enough, the bowl was on its way to the next person.

"Ayden worked there a couple of years ago, and he quit when he noticed some...Well, the place isn't sanitary. The man working the line, he still works there by the way, Ayden. He was picking his nose and eating his buggers while putting lettuce on my sand—"

"Good Christ." He nodded at her when she spoke. "I'm assuming Joey is his name. You said something to him about it."

"No, I said something to that dumbass—not very smart woman working the cash register. She told me that's the special sauce that makes your *buggers,* then she acted like she slipped up and called them burgers so good. I told her that I wanted to see the manager and she told me that it's your—pardon me, your juices as the female manager that makes the fries so crispy."

She didn't get it at first, but the older woman, Brogan, she said her name was, stood up and sat down twice before she asked Lica if he was joking. He said that he'd never joke about something so sexual with a stranger. Then she got it.

Brandy backed from the table so quickly that she nearly fell backward. If not for Lica and his brother on either side of her catching her, she would have hurt herself badly. As it was, she was put in the position of having her head between her knees again and thought she'd be better off staying there this time.

"We're losing business. Well, I guess I know

why now." She sat up and looked at Lica. "What on earth made her think that she could talk to you like that?" His face turned pink, and she thought it suited him, but she didn't make a comment. "So you've dated her before this."

"Good Christ, no. She's...what is she about fifteen? No. Christ, no." She laughed, and he growled. "I used to babysit her when she was a baby. I guess...she makes comments like that to all of us when she sees us. I don't usually engage with her, but I was giving Rodeo another chance after so long and was starving. Not that hungry to eat there, but that's what happened."

"There's more if you want to know about it. If Joey is still working there, I'm betting that none of the other stuff has been taken care of either." She told Ayden she didn't want to know right then. "Good. That's good. It's all worse, by the way. What I would do if I were you is close the place down, fire everyone, and blow the restaurant out of the town. No one will ever eat there again if it gets out that someone said those things and upset Lica." She looked at Lica and asked him why him.

"Because I don't usually comment about things I like or dislike." The older man at the end of the table agreed with Lica. Even going so far as to say that his word was his bond, too. And everyone knew it. "Thank you, Mr. Bates. That means a great deal to me."

No more was said about her employees, and she dug into her meal. Suddenly hungry, she tasted the mashed potatoes and moaned. They were the best thing she'd eaten in a very long time. But then Lica stiffened up and dropped his fork in his mashed potatoes and gravy, which splattered all over her face. She turned to look at him, and that's when she realized that he was staring at her.

"What?" The older man laughed as did both the women. She didn't so much as glance in their direction when one of the many Frazier men asked Lica if she was the one. With his nod, she spoke again. "Am I the one what?"

There wasn't any chance for her to get an answer when the front door to the house exploded open. Every person at the table stood up, and she was shoved to the back of the men. Making her way to the front again, she asked what was going on. It was then that she saw a young man with a gun in his belt with two other men who looked like they'd been out trick or treating and hadn't changed.

"What do we have here? A party for the retiree." She didn't know what that meant, so she kept her mouth shut. But Lica asked the man what he wanted. "Didn't you hear? Bates is retiring? He's put it out there that he's not going to be our big bad alpha anymore. Isn't that what this little get-together is about? The retiring alpha?"

"Lincoln?" The man at the other end of the table said that is why he was here. "To retire? Or something else?"

"To see if you'd take over the job." The man with the gun laughed. "I should have known word would get out faster than I could talk to you."

"What you got here, Lica? A bit of pussy?" Her nerves already shot had Brandy punching the man in the face, completely forgetting about the gun. "What the fuck was that for?"

Brandy punched him again, this time knocking him back a foot. He reached for his gun, and Brandy felt the air around her tighten, like right before lightning struck close to you. Not turning around, she took a step back and felt Lica put his hand on her back.

"You'll have respect in this house. Now, I've

told you once and hit you twice. I don't want to hear another remark like that out of your mouth while you're in this house. Do you understand me?" She had no idea where all this bravo was coming from, but she knew that if she backed down now, he'd eat her alive. "I asked you if you understood me."

"Listen here, you fucking cunt." This time, she slapped him. The extra strength that she suddenly had was enough to knock him into the two men behind him and onto the floor. He was shaking his head when she finally turned to look behind her. Then she turned to face the men still on the floor.

"Lica...I'm assuming that he's Lincoln?" He nodded at her. "Yes, I remember now. I'm assuming since he offered you to be the alpha that you're someone that could...are those wolves behind me your brothers?"

"Yes. They're there to protect you." She nodded, then looked at him again. "You're doing just fine, Brandy. I'm here if you need me, but I'm thinking you have this."

"All right." The man got up, and he lunged at her like a child would do to make you flinch. She didn't. Sort of afraid if she did something like

that, the wolves behind her would think she was...
well, she didn't know what they'd think, actually.
"The next time that I have to remind you of your
manners or the lack of them, I'm going to...I'm
going to remove your hand. If you think I'm
kidding, then you're going to be—Lica, he's a wolf
too, I'm guessing. If you think I'm kidding you,
then you're going to be one paw-less wolf."

Before she could figure out what the hell
was wrong with her, taunting a man with a gun,
she turned her back on him and made her way to
the kitchen. She was going in there to be sick, her
belly not cooperating with all this going on one bit.
Getting herself a glass of water, she was drinking
it down when the man and his two idiot friends
came into the kitchen with Lica and his brother
wolves. The other three, Brogan, Lincoln, and his
wife Judy, were the last to join them.

"I've had enough of your bullshit, woman.
When I take this pack over, the first thing I'm
going to do is make an example out of you." Lica
growled, and she saw his own wolf race over his
face and arms. For whatever reason, she was going
to blame it on the insanity of herself; she knew that
if he did shift, then there would be carnage like

never seen before. She told him she wasn't afraid of him. "You should be. Have you ever been bitten by a wolf? I'm going to tear you apart, piece by little piece. Then, when I'm finished with you, I'm going to let any male around have at you."

"If you tear me to little pieces, how will anyone...you know what? Never mind. I don't care. Would you like to know why? Because you're not going to do a thing to me." She picked up the large clever that was on the table and told him to put his hand on the chopping block. When she was finished here, she was going to have her head examined. There was something very wrong with her. "Put your hand right here. I have warned you."

He did it all the while laughing. This was the most surreal thing she'd ever done. When he laughed at her, telling her that he was going to enjoy killing her, she picked up the clever and cut his hand off at the wrist. Just brought the blade down with a hard swing like she'd done this a million times.

It wasn't real, she told herself. Not a bit of what was happening was real. Until the screams started. Then she knew that there really was something wrong with her. She'd just chopped a man's hand off for threatening to kill her.

~*~

Lica didn't move from his stance beside Brandy. He wasn't touching her, knowing on some level if he did, she'd fall apart. His brothers, all of them men now and dressed, were waiting for the police to show up. Brandy hadn't said a word in the last twenty minutes, and he was beginning to worry about her.

"Lica, did you call my parents? They must be worried that I didn't show up for dinner." He told Brandy that he'd called and that he had spoken to her father. "He'll be worried. I don't usually show up late to have dinner with them."

"They're on their way here. My grannie is going to talk to them when they arrive. Do you need anything?" Brandy said she was all right, and he nodded. "I have some whiskey in the cabinet that we use to make fruit cakes. I don't care for it but we make some to sell for some extra cash after Thanksgiving."

"I think you're supposed to make it with rum. Or bourbon. Not whiskey. I don't care for it either, but my dad loves it. You'll have to let him have some when he's here. Do you think that I'm going to prison?" He told her, for the eighth time, that she wasn't going to go to prison. "Thank you for that. But I believe that I killed that man."

"You didn't kill him. I swear to it. He's out there licking his wounds now that he's shifted and has healed up. Remember? I took a bit of his blood?" She nodded and said that she had too. "Yes. You did. You need to know when he's around."

"Yes. He'll come after me now, won't he?" He said he'd never get past him. "You said that before. I don't know why I believe you, but I do. Just…I don't want any of you to get hurt. Did you call my parents?"

Officer Billings came in the back door. It put him right in the middle of everything that was going on, but he was as calm as he had ever been. It was Lincoln that spoke quietly to him about what had happened. He told the officer that Brandy had warned him three times about him disrespecting her house.

"One thing that I've learned in all my years as an officer was not to disrespect a household when you've come uninvited. Having dinner, were you?" Lica hated to admit it, but he was proud of his human mate. He didn't want her, but he was proud of her. "Ms. Brandy, can you tell me what happened here today?"

When Brandy started talking, he stepped back out of her way to let her get it off her chest. If she didn't get to talk, he knew that it would haunt her for the rest of her life at what she'd done. She didn't kill the punk, David James, but he would never heal from the missing paw until he told her, honestly, how sorry he was. The alpha bitch had wounded him.

"I did warn him not to talk like that. We were having a nice dinner until he broke the front door and came in with his two friends. I didn't know if you were told or not, but he had a gun in his belt." Brandy spoke about what happened like she was giving testimony in a court of law. When she looked at him, he had to ask what was being said as he was mesmerized by her calmness. "Lica, he wants to know if you have anything to say."

"Yes. Lincoln Bates asked us to be the alphas of the pack." She didn't deny it even though the words had never been spoken between them, but he knew if he didn't take it now, that Lincoln and his entire family would be dead before the next moon change. As well as most of the pack. That's not to say that he and his family, including Brandy, wouldn't be harmed either. There would be so many deaths if someone came like David James were to come around and challenge Lincoln that they would be finding bodies for decades after the massacre.

"Well, congratulations to the both of you." He was waiting for Brandy to deny it, but she simply walked away. All he did was give a look to his brother Edmond, and he followed her. She was like a fragile flower right now and he didn't care for it. "What are your plans for the pack, Lica? I'm assuming that the two of you will be moving into the alpha's house. It'll be much nicer than the one here with it just being built and all."

"We've not talked about it much. I've only just found Brandy today, and this is something that we have to discuss." He told him congratulations on that as well, and Lica thanked him. "We have a lot of things to talk about. She's human right now, so I'm making sure that she's getting around well. If you'll excuse me."

He found her in the living room. Grannie was there on the couch, and he saw her shake her head slightly before pointing at Brandy. Since he'd been keeping her calm and talking to her most of the evening, he didn't know what his grannie was doing. As soon as he was within a foot of Brandy, she slapped him twice on his face.

"Since I don't want to lose my hand by pissing you off —" The third time she hit him, he staggered back from it. The punch to his chest hurt him badly enough that he was caught without breath and had to hold onto the wall before approaching her again. "What the hell was that for?"

"You fucker. You act like this is no big deal that I've wounded a person that was...if you have my back like I heard you're supposed to do, being the almighty Lica mate to me, then why the fuck did you allow me to cut that man's hand off?" Lica asked her what he was supposed to do. "You should have told me to let him go. You should have done something rather than just stand there while I...I cut his hand off. Like it was nothing."

"It was more than nothing. It was everything. What do you think would have happened had you blown him off and not done as you threatened? Do you think that he would have said that's fine, I'm going to leave now, it's been fun? No, he wouldn't have. And as for the threat, it was the best one you could have come up with. Cutting his hand, removing it like you did, with promises of retaliations if he didn't heed your warning, is now out there for everyone to see that you're not one to fuck with." He looked as his grannie left them in the room. "What do you think he would have done to you had you not done as you promised, Brandy? I know he would have killed you. Right where you stood, he would have pulled out his gun and blown your head off. Then he would have had to kill each and every member of my family because they would have come to your defense. Then he would have gone on a shooting spree that—"

"That's enough, Lica. I think you've made your point." His anger was making him dizzy, and he growled at his brother, Devlin, when he told him to back off. "You hurt her, and I'm going to die trying to kill you. Back off. Now."

He let his beast take him and he ran out of the house by jumping through the window that was over the couch in the living room. Not slowing, he ran as hard as he could through the trees, jumping over anything that dared to get in his way. Without slowing, he hit the waterway that ran through their property and out the other side without a single thought to what he was doing. Running. Not away, but he told himself that he was letting off steam, that was all.

It was dark when he finally stopped. He didn't have any idea where he was, but he knew that he was still on their land. He could smell his brothers and himself, knowing that they'd been out here recently enough cutting wood for the winter that their scent was still fresh. Lying down on the soft grass, he was keen enough to keep an eye out for humans and other creatures while he waited for his heart to slow down enough that he could go home. The scent of Brandy startled him.

"If you shift into a human will—wait, you hate humans. If you shift to your other self, will you be naked?" He told her through their link that since he'd found his mate, he didn't know. "All right. Then I'd like for you to stay the way you are. I have some things to say to you, and I'd very much like it if you let me say it. First of all, I told Lincoln that we would, and the two of us would take over the pack. He said that at some point, when you agree, too, that, we'll get some magic.

I don't know what that entails, but that's what he told me."

"*We'll be more. I'm not sure what that means about you, but I want you to know that I don't hate all humans. Just most of them.*" She looked away, but not before he saw the pain he'd caused her. "*I'm sorry.*"

"Don't be sorry for being honest with me. It might hurt me but that's none of your concern. All right, so you're not sure of what might happen, but I was told that we'd have to have sex and exchange blood while climaxing for us to be mates. Is that right?" Lica told her that he didn't know for sure, but his Grannie would know. "She's not speaking to me right now. I think that I hurt her feelings when I asked her how to get out of being your mate. I guess that it's a done deal unless one of us dies. I'm not ready to die just yet, so I guess we're going to be stuck with each other."

That hurt. He didn't have any idea why it felt like his heart was broken into pieces, but it hurt him to his core. When he asked her what she was thinking, she looked at him for a long time, so long that he didn't think that she was going to answer him.

"I don't like you. I know that it doesn't matter to you one way or the other, but I don't believe that I'll ever want to either. You're a mean person, especially to me when I had nothing to do with what has happened between us. That being said, I'll have sex with you — but absolutely no kissing. We're not in love, nor will we be, and kissing seems so intimate to me, and we're never going to be that way. But with sex? It'll be just the one time to bond or whatever it's called, but I don't want you to come near me again." Again, his heart hurt and he put his paw over the pain to see if his heart was beating still. "There is something else that you should know. I have money. A great deal of it. And as of an hour ago, your name is on all my accounts. Also, I have a couple dozen houses all over the world that also you own with me." He started to speak, but she cut him off. "Don't tell me that you don't want any of it. Because if you don't have all that I have, I won't help your brothers either. And I like them a great deal more than you. So, do I call my attorney or not to change it from our name to just mine."

"*No.*" She told him he was a smart person. He wasn't nearly as pissed off at her than he thought he should have been. *"And I agree with you. Absolutely no, not ever kissing. Not even for show. No kissing. As for money? We have very little money. Not even enough that we could live off of for the rest of the month. There is pack money, too, as well as money that will be paid to us monthly. But I don't know how much or how much we're to get paid when it's time."*

"All right. You've made your point about kissing. Money? You don't need it. We don't need it, I mean." He asked her how much money she was talking about if they didn't need the monthly to pay them for being pack alpha's. "Billions of dollars. Not including houses, stocks, bonds, businesses and anything else that you can think of. And I own the Rodeo Burger company. There are five thousand restaurants across the United States You do as well. So, do you want to have sex out here or in a bed someplace? As I said, I have a house, it's close to here."

He got up and shifted. Lica was glad that he was clothed, but he wasn't thrilled about the callus way she was treating him about sex. Walking by her, he made his way back to the house, and he knew when she turned and followed him. He could feel her pain, her heart hurting, but he couldn't do anything about it. His own was shattered as well. The thing was, he didn't understand why. She'd been right on all the stuff that she'd said. They didn't even like one another, didn't get together, but because they'd been fated. But her talking about sex like it was a duty—he caught himself when he thought that. Because that's exactly what she was saying, too. It was a duty for them to have sex. So that he could take over the pack and be able to run it safely. Christ, he wished he'd never met her. Sort of.

She was treating him the same way that he'd been treating her. Cold indifference. He no more wanted her than she did him, apparently. When he was ready to go into the house, he turned to her and asked her if she wanted to sleep here or someplace else. She didn't say a word but went into the house and into the living room. When she got onto the couch, a lumpy piece of shit that had come with the home, he sat on the other couch. After she pulled the blanket that had seen better days off the back and laid down. He supposed he deserved whatever he got from her.

Reaching out to Lincoln, he told him that he'd take the pack. As soon as he laid down, he felt the magic roll painfully over him. He would have gone to Brandy, too, he didn't know, to help her when she started screaming, but it was too late for both of them. They were getting the magic that came with his new position as the new pack alphas.

Chapter 4

Alan watched his daughter as she sat at her desk, making decisions right and left like she had met her mate every day, and it was no big deal. He knew a bit more about being a mate to a wolf than he had a few weeks ago. He had several shifters working for him, and they'd been very helpful in giving him information, more than his daughter would have if he were to question her about it. His employees were very forthcoming too about the information about her being mated to an alpha than he bet Lica knew. The way the two of them went about, he would wonder if the rumor was true, that the two of them would be powerful alphas. For the most part, the two of them ignored each other more than anything.

Alan wanted it to work for them both. He enjoyed Lica's company, and he so wanted his daughter's happiness. Brandy finally looked up at him. Her eyes looked glazed over just a little, but then she smiled at him.

"How long have you been here, Dad? Did I miss a meeting with you?" He said that he'd not been here long, only a few minutes, when he knew it was closer to an hour. "What's up? I'm trying to catch up on the things I missed while I was resting." So that's what she was calling it when she and Lica had been knocked cold while getting the magic? Resting.

"Yes, you were resting for a few days. It worried your mother and me a bit, but we were assured that the two of you were just fine." It had taken him an entire day to get over the fact that his daughter was now going to be magical. Then he'd gone to his closet and— "Did I tell you that I can change my clothing with a thought? Scared me a little bit, I'll have to admit but your mom loves it. She said she's never going to have to go shopping for evening gowns again."

Brandy laughed with him, but she was distracted. He could see that, so he tried tripping her up so that he could get to the bottom of whatever was bothering her. He asked her if she had picked out the raccoons for the backyard display. He was sure that her distraction had to do with Lica and her being mated to him, but he liked the young man. As well as all of his family.

"The raccoons come around on their own, thank you very much. I'm paying attention, Dad. I just have a lot to—I took Ayden's advice on the local Rodeo. I got rid of everyone who worked there and denied them unemployment. Which I can do because they were a public hazard—Dad, everyone was in on that entire gross food catastrophe so I closed the place down. It was torn down yesterday, and I've put the land up for sale. Ayden suggested that if it doesn't sell, put something else there that has nothing to do with food." Alan loved that idea and told her so. "I'll wait a few years and then open something else around here. I've had offers on the land, but I'm holding out until the place is cleaned up. People might not like that it was such a terrible place to... well, eat. Since it's in a good location, I think it will be worth more after a couple of years anyway."

"You made us rich by having wonderful

ideas like that one. What are you going to do with Ayden? I don't know why, but I have a feeling that he's going to be working for you soon." She told him that she hired him a few days ago, and he was going to be an undercover shopper for her. "If you don't just mean him going to Rodeo's, that's a lot of traveling, but I think that he'll enjoy it."

"He was so excited to get his passport that I thought he was going to dance around the room to celebrate. The officers certainly found it to be funny. He's supposed to be picking out him a smallish building to work from here as a base operation, or he can work from home. I suggested that he find himself a place from home so he can have a down time place to go." After she told him about hiring the other brothers for different projects she had going, neither of them mentioning Lica, he asked her about the cattle ranch. "I don't have anything to do with that. Since Lica and I don't talk all that much, he doesn't bring me in on any decisions that he makes on that side. I'm all right with that. I know about as much as he does in having a corporate meeting with the few shareholders we have. It's working out for us for now."

It wasn't, and he knew it. His little girl was

sad, not always, but most of the time. He talked to her about the two ventures that they were both in on, and she seemed to have a handle on those as well. The only thing was her personal life, and it was in the shitter, as Brogan was fond of saying.

They'd always been close, the three of them. Her mom was better at talking to Brandy about boys—well, he supposed men now, but how would one start a conversation about a man that you'd basically been married to because of him not being a human. Shaking his head a little, he looked at his baby girl.

"Honey, I'm worried about you." She turned away, but not before he could see the hurt in her eyes. "Want me to have a talk with Lica? Figure out what's going to be going on with the two of you? I don't know what is wrong, but you being sad all the time is really breaking my heart."

"I'm all right, Dad. Really. And no, I don't want you talking to Lica. If he has something to say to me, I know that he'll come to tell me. Thank you, but we're doing just what needs to be done. We've not had sex, I guess that will mean that we've bonded or something and make us stronger, but I have no intention of doing it the one time for that to happen. I told him that, too. He seemed all right with it as well." They'd always been able to talk to Brandy about a lot of things, sex, however, knowing that she was mated to the big wolf embarrassed him like it never had before. "I guess you could say that we're coexisting. Not really, since he's staying at the ranch house and I'm at my home, but it's working out for us. I just wish he'd get it over with so that I can move on. I'm as nervous as a cat in a room of rockers. I got that from Brogan."

Alan laughed when she did. There wasn't anything funny about what she'd said. He knew more than most that knew his daughter that she had always been good at covering up her feelings better than most. Even her happiness, short-lived as it was nowadays, was something that she didn't share with many people.

"Brandy Conner-Fraizer." He'd forgotten that she was calling herself Fraizer now. It startled him that she would be so casual about it, too, when the phone rang and she answered it that way. When she asked who was on the other end of the call if she could put it on speaker phone, they must have agreed. "My dad is here now. Go ahead, Edmond. Tell us what you think of the new shop that is going in town. Wait, let me give him a little bit of back history with it.

"A place that I was looking at for some office space has been rented out. The man at the downtown offices of land transfers said that he didn't know what they were doing but they're saying that it will bring in five thousand new jobs. That seemed odd to me because the building can't hold five hundred people, much less five thousand. So Edmond said he'd go and check it out for us." She asked her dad if he needed more. "Okay, Edmond, we're both ready now."

"It's a scam. Everything about the place is a red flag. I tried the phone number to call in for jobs, and they wanted my bank account information so that they could prove I was a real person. I hope no one here falls for that. I went by here today, and all the doors and windows are papered up so that you can't see inside the place to see what is going on. But I didn't let the 'no trespassing' signs give me too much trouble and I got inside. There is nothing going on in here that would have me thinking they'll be ready for their grand opening in four days. The entire first floor looks like it did ten years ago when the shop closed down. The boxes that we noticed coming off the trucks are just stacked up in one corner like they're waiting on someone to open them." Alan asked if there were any names on the boxes. "Good point. Let me look. Hang on, Lica's here too. He's got a knife we can use."

Just a glance at Brandy made him realize that she had tensed up. She laid the phone down on the desk and got up to go to the fridge. It was very telling to him that she was getting as far from the phone as she could, and thusly, Lica. He told them the name on the boxes.

"It sounds as if they were just taken out of random trash bins. Wait. They're full of some kind of merchandise. Here's one that's for the ranch that has lubricant in it for the cattle." They could hear boxes being wrestled around and it made him nervous a little that they were in a building that didn't belong to them. "Is Brandy there with you, Alan?" He said that she was. "Brandy, did you order something from a catalog and it didn't turn up at your home?"

"Yes. It was supposed to have...let me look." She went to her desk and opened her computer. "Yes. It's signage that goes out front of the property that we've just closed up. Not the Rodeo but a diner that had been losing money for decades. Is the box there?"

"There are several full boxes here for different addresses around town. Two for you. One for the ranch. A couple for a couple of neighbors. All of them are open, but the items are still in the box. I think I've figured out what's going—"

"What the fucking hell are you doing in here? This is private property." Lica told them to call the police. The people had shown up with guns. As soon as he hung up, Brandy did just what she was told. Sending them to the building, saying that there were guns involved, she grabbed her jacket and asked him if he was going.

"Yes. Of course." They were out the door and running across the street, arriving before the police arrived. Four cruisers pulled up just as there was gunfire. He didn't want her to go inside, but she was nearly in the doorway when the gunfire sounded. Alan directed the police inside and told them who was inside. Christ, this was going to be trouble for someone.

The talking to him link thing made him

jump every time someone used it to talk to him. His wife said the same thing. It was as if someone had snuck up behind them to scare you. But this time, he knew the voice. Lica told him that he and Brandy had been walking along to the store and heard the noise. Nothing more but to keep their mouth about anything else unless he tells them.

They were both asked the same question, why were they there. He might well have said that they were looking around, but he said just what he was told to say. It was Lica who started talking that, making it sound like they were just passing by, and he heard his wife.

"Some of these boxes are hers, and I was just wondering about that." The man in cuffs, down on his knees with two other men, asked why he thought they'd be in this building. "But they were in here, weren't they? You can't dispute that. Even something from the ranch. I've called the company complaining about not receiving it when it's been just sitting here all this time. This isn't the address that I gave them to send me my things. I doubt very much if any of these people's merchandise had been shipped here. I'll have to go home and look, but I have cameras there. I'd like to see how they —"

"He's lying. We looked hard. There ain't no cameras anywhere around that ugly farmhouse. Not her business either." The officer asked his daughter if she had cameras. "I just told you that she didn't."

"We have cameras all around the building. Remember when I came to you last month and had our company set up in a specialized room for you to watch over after hours? While I don't know when my boxes were taken, you can bet that there is a recording of it on the back cameras to see what happened." The man on the floor just started cursing. It was hilarious to him that the man, even with all the evidence they had on him, kept telling Brandy that he'd looked for cameras while he'd been stealing and hadn't found any at all. Finally, it was Lica who told him to shut his mouth.

After that, all three of the men were arrested. Lica and Edmond were admonished about entering buildings where they weren't supposed to go but also thanked for finding the porch pirates that had the police baffled for the last several months. He thought it was a good day all the way around.

Alan said that he was hungry and would

buy them all lunch, even the two cops if they joined them. The officers declined, as he knew they would, but Lica and Edmond said that they were hungry, and his daughter said she'd come too. He thought that it was a win-win for all of them.

~*~

Lica hadn't been able to eat out as much as he was since he and Brandy had found each other. It was a blast also for him to be able to just go into any place and order whatever was on the menu. He didn't do that, of course. Even with her having billions and billions of dollars, he knew that in order to keep that much coming in, they'd have to cut corners even now. He cleared his throat to ask about the cameras that he didn't have around the ranch.

"Cost? Well, if we find someone to come out and put the system in for us, and one cow or whatever it is you're worried about gets stolen, then it will make the cost worth it, correct? I mean, how much do you lose if one, dollars to dollars when something comes up missing...I don't know what you do, so I can't figure out a price per whatever." He told her, thinking it was funny that she was willing to tell him she didn't know anything. "Okay. So, a standing on the hoof cow would weigh in at about twelve hundred pounds. Christ, that's a lot of steak."

"We sell on the hoof. Which means that they weigh the steer while it's still alive and standing on its own. Each one will cost per pound that way. One of the reasons that we've never butchered our cattle for the public is that you have to have a slaughterhouse that is inspected every few months. Not that we're not clean where we sell our meat, but this was an inexpensive way for us to raise our cattle and then make a profit, too." She asked him if they made any profit at all in doing this. "Yes. Not as much as most jobs, but it kept us in food and a roof over our heads for the last few years. Here, let me explain it to you the way that I learned it. Say your dad came to buy a steer, take it to his own butcher and have it cut up to suit his needs. But, and this happens no matter who does the butchering on a twelve hundred pound steer, your dad is going to lose weight. About four hundred and fifty pounds of the weight will be skin, some bones, and hoof."

"That's a great deal. I had no idea that you'd lose so much after the work is done. Then, what do they do with...I don't want to know, I don't think." Alan laughed and asked him if he'd someday like to get into butchering cattle. "I mean, if the opportunity came along, would you do a few cattle a year for family and whatnot."

"I can do it for our family. That's how we get our own meat. But since I'm not selling it to anyone but for our own personal use, then it only needs to have the meat inspected, not the place...I'm sure they have standards that they want things to be but they've never said anything to us about it." Alan asked if he could have a tour when Brandy apologized about having to take a call and left them there. When she stepped outside, he said he was going to make sure she was all right. He heard his brother explaining about what had happened to them early this morning.

Lica didn't go far just outside the door to keep an eye on her. Leaning against his truck, he just watched her. He could tell that she was frustrated. Whether it was about him or the call, however, he didn't know. But he wasn't going to leave her out here alone. Once she hung up, she was pissed. He could see and then heard it in her voice when she spoke to him.

"What the hell are you doing? That was a private call." He said he was keeping an eye on her. "You don't think that I can take care of myself? Am I going to have to expect you to—"

"The young man that you saved us from, David James, is making noises about finding you and killing you." That shut her up and had her looking around. "He's out of jail, as are his two buddies. They're looking for you so that they can get revenge for what you did. Did anyone explain to you that his wrist will not heal until he apologizes to you? He has to mean it, too."

"No. I mean, someone might have said that when he...I wasn't exactly listening very well after I removed his hand. I wake up in the middle of the night screaming when I think about what I did to him." He told her that she was justified in what she'd done. "Then why do I feel so horrible for doing it? I do, just so you know."

"I know that we've not had a great deal of time to talk about what's happened between us, the sharing of magic. There is some rule about the magic that allowed you to, and Brandy, the magic did allow you to remove his hand to save us. But if it wasn't justified in what you did, then the wound would have healed up immediately. As it stands right now, it's an open wound. Not even the best doctors in the world can seal it up so that it heals. He needs to talk to you calmly and tell you how very sorry he is for what he did to make you have to remove his hand." She asked him if that was true. Not that she would blame him for lying about this to make her feel better, but she would rather he didn't lie about the magic. "I'm telling you the truth. And it's because you're more powerful than he is. That's something else you should know. You are by far more powerful than any wolf or human out there. You're the alpha bitch, and he knew it when he came here to challenge me."

"Then I should have let you do it." He shook his head, but before he could tell her, she spoke to him. "While I don't want people, anyone, to cross the street because I'm coming down the same sidewalk, I know it's because word has gotten around to other shifters, so they know what I did. The cook at my home is a wolf. I didn't know that until the other morning, but she said that she was so proud to be working for the Alpha and his bitch. Then she told me that all the males and females alike were proud of me for saving the household when James showed up. I don't think that's a terrible thing, do you?"

"No. So long as someone doesn't get it into their head to challenge you. Not that I don't think you can take care of yourself, but you'll have to make sure that you're not alone. Please? If someone harms you in any way, they'll be dead. And it will not be an easy death either. And it more than likely will not be me. For as much as I've heard from the pack about you, there are only about five that wouldn't lay down their lives for you. Me too, she said, but mostly for you. I'm second only to you because you may someday breed a son or daughter for me. Not my words but theirs." She paced back and forth, and he watched her. This was only the third time in the six weeks that he'd known about her that he'd spent any time with her alone. He wondered what she was thinking and then decided that it wouldn't bode well for him to look. So he asked her what she was thinking.

"I would like to carry a gun. I don't know if I could use it on another person, but if a wolf comes after me, I want to be able to at least slow them down so that I can get away or get some help." He handed her the one that was in the back of his pants. It was the main reason that he wore a vest, so he could cover his weapon up. "Thank you." She looked at him. "Aren't you afraid that I'll use it on you?"

"No. I don't think I'm afraid you will. You could, I guess, but according to shifter law, you're not supposed to be able to hurt me." She asked him about his parents. "That's a good thought. My parents hurt one another and us all the time. I think you have a point. I knew, someplace in the back of my head, that they shouldn't have been able to hurt us. I think that the fates that put them together...You know, I don't have an answer for that."

"The fates did what they did to make you into the men that you are today. If not for your childhood and the exact way that you were brought up, I don't believe that any of you would be the men, good men that you are today." She looked around and then went to the door. "I'm hungry, and I would guess that our food is there."

She went into the restaurant, and he stood there leaning against the truck. If he didn't know any better, he'd say that she complimented him and his brothers. Grabbing the door handle to the restaurant, he went inside smiling. She'd put him off guard again. He was going to have to be on his toes if he was going to hang out with her all that often."

When he was seated, he was happy to see that the staff was bringing out the food. His sandwich, well, both of them, were hot from the oven, and he couldn't have been happier. Once the server left them to get refills on drinks, he handed the other gun he had in his pants to Alan. He tried to give it back, and Brandy told him to keep it.

"What would you do if you're out with Mom and that idiot three-paw comes after the two of you because he wants me?" Lica asked if she was going to call David three-paw from now on. "Yes. I think that's a good name for the despicable person. I would rather you carry the gun all the time, even around the house, Dad. Having a gun that you can't get to or use because you didn't want to carry it means that you're dead. I don't want that any more than you'd want for me. Right?"

"Yes. I never thought of it that way. I'm betting your mother will put up a fuss." Lica asked Alan if she'd be upset if he was carrying. "Oh no. Not her. Debra will be upset that she wasn't asked to have one as well. My wife, she's very protective of us. More so than I think a bear with her cubs. No, she'll be going out and getting herself one as well."

"Here, let her have this one." Edmond winked at Brandy when she looked at him. "I have another one at home. Since I'm with all of you, I'll be good until I get to my other one. But you give her that one. It's a Glock, so she should be able to kill whatever she needs. Also, I don't know if Lica mentioned this to you or not, but the bullets are all silver. So they'll kill a vampire as well."

Lica laughed. The more he gave thought to the conversation that they were having, the harder he laughed. They were all talking about guns and the creatures they might have to kill with one, like they were on some kind of death squad. And he was having a blast. He might not want or need a mate, but he sure did enjoy her family. They were very cautious and went with the flow like people he'd never met before.

After they were finished up eating, Alan said that he had to finish up some paperwork at the office before he made his way home. Brandy said the same, that she had to read over one more contract that was for a loan before the morning. She had a meeting with their corporate heads at nine tomorrow. Just as she was about to cross the road, she stopped and turned to him.

"This meeting is something that I don't do all that often. I mean, we don't load money to people but usually buy stock. But we might, and that's a big might be lending him the capital to expand. If you'd like to come, you'll be very welcome." He nodded and asked her what he should wear. "Do you have a dress suit?"

"No. I mean, I have one, but I don't think it fits as well as it used to." She said for him to wear some jeans and a nice white shirt if he had one with a tie. "All right. Do you think that I should purchase a suit for things like this?"

"Yes. All of you will need a few suits. I'll set up a tailor for you and your brothers tonight." He asked if they needed it to be tailored. "Yes. If you're going to a business meeting, first impressions are always the best. Lenord, he's the man that does my dad's suits. He might have one he can fix up for you for in the morning but you'll be all right if he doesn't. I'll let the others know when they can be suited up."

He went with her to her office. It wasn't anywhere he'd been before, and he was glad that she introduced him as her husband. Ten minutes after she sat behind her desk and picked up her phone, a man by the name of Lenord Salva showed up and took him to the other room.

Christ, he was embarrassed to have to get measured; he thought that man knew every single part of his body and how long it had been. He told him that Lica would never be able to look good in anything but a tailored suit and that he would be the only one who could make him one. Lica had no idea what that meant but he did feel strange when he found out his leg length.

That measurement made him squeak. He decided right then and there that he wasn't going to tell his brothers about this. He was going to let them learn about it all on their own. And he was going to make sure that he was there when the time came for them to be measured too. Especially Edmond. Edmond didn't care to be touched. From their childhood, he figured it was going to be a blast watching him answer the question, 'Do you hang on the left or right' and see if he knew what it meant. Yes, he thought, this was going to be a lot of fun.

Chapter 5

"What?" Brandy had to pull her eyes away from Lica when he came into her office. Good lord, if he looked this good with well-fitting clothing on, then naked, he'd be, "Brandy, is something wrong with what I'm wearing?"

"No. I just never thought of you in a suit before." He grinned, and she turned her back to him. "You're more of a jeans person like I've seen you wear since I've met you. But Lenord was correct. A suit off the rake would never hang on you, right."

Embarrassed when he laughed, she went into the conference room off from her office and started putting the files in front of each chair that was set close to the long table. He asked if he could help, and she pointed to where the bottled water was and asked him to put them on the table.

Brandy could only carry about four, maybe five bottles of water to the table. Lica picked up the case in one hand and used his free one to set the bottles where she told him. Then he put out napkins to go under them when he found a stack of them, too. Having him around was going to be helpful in so many ways, she thought to herself. He asked her if she had a moment that he could talk to her.

"I have two questions for you. One, I'm not in a hurry to get an answer, but the second one is, do you want me to have any opinions in this meeting? Am I going to be—not being mean but like a boy toy to you while here? I didn't mean boy toy. I meant a heavy, someone to keep you safe. The way you looked at me when I got here, that's what made me think of the—never mind. My mouth got ahead of my head, and I apologize for that. The first question is about getting cameras set up around the ranch to keep an eye on the cattle." She asked him if he'd ever been to a business meeting. "Just when I get turned down for a loan. The banker here, Howard Slaven, he won't allow our kind to open an account unless it's for a business. Even then, he's very particular about what we take the money out for. I don't know why but that's just what he does. I sometimes wonder if he has a list of all the shifters in town and keeps a daily accounting of their accounts. I don't know, I guess that's silly."

"He needs a good swift kick to his head is what he needs. When I was putting money in yours and your brothers' accounts, he didn't have anything to do with it because I did it on line. I wonder what he would have said to me had I come in and done it." Lica told her that he simply wouldn't allowed her to do it. "So it's doubtful that he knows the balance to your accounts."

"I would say that's about right. And speaking of money, I know that you told me that I didn't have to come to you for money, but I would very much like it if I came to you when the amount is over a certain dollar amount." She stopped and turned to look at him, asking him why. "Well, I know nothing about the accounts you've put me on. I know you told me that I have as much buying power as I need, but I don't want you to pull up a statement and flip out because I spent five hundred grand."

"Okay, I guess I would like to know that. And I'm not saying that if you need it, you don't spend it until you talk to me. What would that be for? You can do it, but I think you're right. A heads up would be good." He told her what he wanted to do. "Yes, that's wonderful. But we need to set you up a business account for the ranch instead of taking it out of the personal accounts. There is plenty enough to cover a check that size, but it should come out of business for tax reasons."

"I never thought of that." She said she'd get him with an attorney today for them to sit and set the account up. "Thank you. And I do appreciate you allowing me to—"

"I'm not *allowing* you to do anything, Lica. You are, I guess, my partner—an equal partner in all things the same as I'm yours. However, the money is for all of us. You're also running a business that I know absolutely nothing about. However, numbers I can work with. At the end of this deal today, for example. If, as I said, that's a big deal, if we lend this company money, it's going to be in the millions. Seven or eight. Then there is the loan that we're going to work with that will be nearly that much more to expand his business. While I trust that you'll use the money for what you say you will, and there is no need for you to worry that I won't trust you, but this man? I feel something slimy from him. Like...I don't know. Like, he's going to get the money to expand, but there is a shiny thing right there in the corner that he really wants, and no one will care if he uses a bit of it for that. It's happened before."

"Speaking of shiny objects, I have a ring for you. It wasn't my mother's ring. I don't even know if my parents were really married, but my grannie gave it to me, and I had it sized for you with help from your dad." He handed it to her, and she felt hurt by that. It was in a box, but that's as far as he went in asking her or telling her that he wasn't going to put much effort into winning her heart. Not that she wanted him to have—. "I thought about doing the whole down on one knee thing, but since I know that we're only doing this for show, you wouldn't like that either."

She turned her back on him and made her way to the cupboard to grab some pens for the table and to hide her pain while slipping the ring and box into her pocket. He asked her if she was all right. And she told him that she needed to get forty notepads from her secretary so they'd have enough to go around. While he did that, she laid the pens on the table and hurried to her bathroom.

Brandy didn't have any idea why she was upset by the way he gave her the ring. He'd been right in saying that this was a sham of a marriage and the only reason they were even together was because someone somewhere had picked her out of a crowd and gave her to Lica. He needed them to have sex so that he'd be more powerful, magically powerful, to run the pack. And she was going to do that without complaint. Also, she wasn't going to be stingy with the money that she had going into this sham, either. If she were going to be like that, it would be harder for both families. Especially his. They weren't going to go down the tubes if she—

"Brandy, your phone is ringing on your desk. Do you want me to get it?" She told him to go ahead, and she'd be out in a moment. "All right."

Fixing her face, something that her own grannie used to say to her all the time, she looked in the mirror hard. Her nose was a little bit red, and her lipstick was a little lighter than it was when she came in. Thanks to washing her face, she was ready to get on with her life. Anyway, she could muddle through it, she supposed. Brandy opened the door and nearly fell into the arms of Lica, who was just standing there.

"What do you think you're doing coming out of there — what's happened?" She told him that he was the one lurking around behind her bathroom door, or she wouldn't have fallen. "You've been crying. Which person did it so that I can have a talk with them?"

"You." He glared at her, and she welcomed that over him, laughing at her. "You're making me insane, and sometimes you make me cry. Because you're acting like this…this thing between us can be put off forever. Well, I'm getting sick of waiting on you to make a decision." A voice clearing had her turning to her right. Her dad was standing there with one of the clients. "I'm sorry, Dad, Mr. Green. I've not had a good week. That's no excuse to take it out on Lica, but…well, no buts, I've had a bad day, and he was the one in line to get blasted."

Brandy didn't bother apologizing to Lica. She could see the anger on his face, and she didn't want to deal with it today. She'd not lied when she said she was having a terrible day. What she didn't say was that he'd been the one that had put her in it. She didn't want to deal with him on one of her good days either. But he would need to get his sex thing over with so that she wasn't forever thinking what a colossal mistake this has been agreeing to be his mate.

By the time all the men for the meeting had shown up, she was worked up again. This time, it was her nerves and had nothing to do with Lica. He was keeping his distance, for which she was grateful, but it didn't help that there were fifty-four men in her conference room. Forty-one of them were attorneys, and they were all screaming at her to answer their questions first and foremost.

The shrill whistle came from her left. Looking at Lica, she could tell that he was as frustrated as she was with the men. Neither of them had gotten a word out of welcoming before they started yelling.

"Now. The next person, I don't care which side of the table you're from, ours or theirs. If you say a word, I'm going to have you escorted out of this building. If you think for one moment that I'm kidding or that you don't think I can do that, then try me. I'm in just as shitty mood as my wife is. Do you, quietly and with a raise of your hand, understand what it is that I've said to you?" Everyone raised their hands, and she nearly laughed when one man on the other end of the table from them raised his hand and frantically waved it at her and Lica. "You'll have your turn to speak in a moment. Unless the building is on fire, put your hand down and be quiet."

"What is the meaning of this man talking to me like this?" While she told Mr. Green that Lica was her husband and her partner so he could say what he wanted, Lica said he was calling security. "I'm in charge of this meeting, and I demand respect."

"No, we're in charge of this meeting, and you'll sit there and do as you're told, or this meeting is finished. I told you from the very beginning that I wasn't going to put up with your shenanigans around here, Mr. Green. I'm working with you, but I will quit, and you know that I don't lie when it comes to this company. I will have you tossed out of this building, and we'll never do any business again." Mr. Green stood up. The attorney on either side of him pulled at the older man, trying to get him to sit down. "Do it, Mr. Green, and this will be —"

"I'm not going to allow you to bully me around. This is my company until I say differently." She asked him what he meant. "I'm going to show you how to run a successful business, and you're going to shut up and sit down. I have the terms I'm willing to work with all written out. Now, be a good girly and sign where you're supposed to, and we'll get this finished with or without your help."

"Lica." That's all she had to say that got him moving. He stood behind Mr. Green's chair and pulled it from the long table. The two attorneys stood up, began gathering the things they'd only just sat out, and were talking to the people around them. Security asked Mr. Green if he wanted to be standing when he left or if he wanted to be carried out. She was not fucking around today. Apparently, neither was Lica.

"You're bluffing. There is no way that you can afford to turn me down for business." Security, with the help of Lica, started pulling Green and some of the people who simply followed him out toward the doors. "I'm going to own your business by the end of the day, young lady. You see that I don't."

"You can't even keep your own company afloat, how do you think that we're going to take you seriously that you'll be taking this one. My wife has been running this business in the black since she opened the doors. She pays her taxes on time, her employees' retirement accounts are all up to date, and she's not spent any money on doodads like you have in order to keep up with the neighbors. You've been running in the red since the year your father-in-law turned the reins over to you when you married his daughter. I bet that Mr. Bierut has regretted it since. Mr. Green, as it stands right now, we're not going to help you with a loan or the expansion. I know for a fact that you've been turned down by four other institutions since you've been caught not paying into your employees' retirement accounts."

"Where did you get that information? You've no right to be snooping around in things that are of no concern of yours. For all you know, I was going to pay that back with some of the money that you are going to loan me. You and that ditzy wife of yours." She didn't even see Lica move, but she knew that it had to have been him that hit the man. Mr. Green's head slammed back into the wall behind him, and blood splattered all over the men in front of him. "You've hit me. My god, you've broken my nose. Did any of you see that? Did you see that he hit me? I told him I was going to own him, and now I am."

"I didn't see anything, Green. Perhaps on your way home, you should make an appointment with your eye doctor. You tripped, that's all." One of the attorneys looked at her. He was smiling. "Mrs. Frazier, if you don't mind, I'll be calling you later. Ms. Green, Mr. Green's daughter has taken over the company as of the moment her father left the building. Mr. Fraizer was correct. Mr. Bierut was regretful of his son-in-law taking his company. He posthumously handed it over to her when she turned twenty-one with all kinds of money to keep the business from falling apart. She would like to get with you and your husband to help her set up a business plan that will work for years to come. Thank you too for the day."

After they all left, she sat down in her office. Brandy wasn't the least bit surprised when Lica joined her by sitting across the desk from her. Smiling, she asked him how he knew about the employee funds and the daughter.

"His daughter, Elisa, called to speak to me last evening, and she's been helping me with information that we could use against her father. I guess he doesn't believe women, and this is solely on him, are strong enough to run a company, much less deal with money." Lica stood up where her secretary brought in a tray with a pot of tea and two dainty looking cups and saucers on it with several kinds of cookies on a plate. He sat it on the edge of her desk after taking it from her secretary. "She has known since she was ten that she'd be taking over the company. That's about the time that he was messing with the retirement funds. She's been learning everything she could about the company from her grannie. Who ran the company with her grandda before her father did."

"Thank you. For the information, help, and the cup of tea." She sipped hers quietly and closed her eyes. "I've been stressed out for the last few hours. Mr. Green started calling my home around seven last night and didn't stop while I drove to work. I was going to turn him down anyway, but this was so much slicker."

If Lica answered her in anyway, she didn't hear him. At some point, he told her that she should rest, and she thought that she objected, but her tea cup was taken away and a warm blanket wrapped around her. That was all she remembered of the meeting. Brandy thought that if she could rest for a few minutes, she'd feel much better.

~*~

Lica knocked on the door. He had thought about just walking in, Brandy had told him that his name was on this house, too, but that felt wrong somehow, so he knocked a second time. He was thoroughly surprised when a man dressed in a livery of the same blue as the shutters on the house were opened the door.

"Mr. Fraizer, I presume." He told the man that he was one of six of them. "Yes, she showed us pictures of all of your brothers but for yourself. She didn't have a single one, I'm afraid. Come in, sir. Mrs. Fraizer is upstairs. There was a bit of a snafu this afternoon, and she's up there now trying her best not to fire a few people."

"I'll go see if I can help. I need to speak to her anyway." Taking the stairs two at a time, he was surprised at not just the elegance of the house but the sheer expense of everything. And he'd only entered the front of the house. The handrailing alone would cost more than he'd made in the last year. It was a double-wide staircase that dropped you off at a landing as big as his living room. Then, it split into two to go to either end of the household by way of a long, wide hallway. He heard her voice down the right hallway and made his way there.

She was indeed into something. While he didn't know exactly what was going on, he knew that someone was going to be fired by the time it was finished. The towels, there had to be two hundred of them were lined up in piles along the wall in stacks of four. There were other things, too, such as hand towels and what he thought were some kind of finger towels. He'd never read up on what towels were used for when he'd been made aware of just how much money Brandy had and what sort of dinners they might host. Thank god for her father was all he could think about. She saw him about the time he was nearing the end of the towels.

"Do you see this? This is what happens when I'm stressed out." He told her she was very stressed. "Are you making fun of me? I'll let you know that I'm in a rotten mood, and you teasing me isn't the thing to do."

"I'm not teasing you at all. But you're not the only one that is stressed." He put his hands on her shoulders and turned her to the five women and one man who were standing against the wall behind her like they were lined up for a firing squad. "Who is responsible for the towels? I'm assuming that it's what has you stressed."

"I am." She didn't move, but he continued holding her shoulders to start massaging them. "I ordered them. And for the life of me I don't know why I'm taking it out on these nice people."

"I would think that it's fine, right?" He nodded, and each of the others nodded, too. "Where are these towels supposed to be going?"

"There should have been a different color for each bathroom. But they're all this light gray." He asked the young man what the problem was then. "The missus, Brandy, your missus usually has a different color for each room. But they're all this color and none to put in the other bathrooms."

"Okay. Good information." Brandy turned in his arms and laid her head on his shoulder. There weren't many women who could reach his shoulder, so he was thrilled—he didn't know why—to have her there. "Let's do this so we don't have to send them all back. Each bathroom will now have gray towels. That way, I'm assuming that they won't have to be divided by colors all the time to be put away. Correct?"

"That's what your missus said she was going to do." Brandy nodded but didn't lift her head off his shoulder. "She said that it would make it easier to sort things. We were agreeing with her when you showed up. But then she started to cry, and it threw us off. Ms. Brandy never cries. I think she might be ill."

"I think that she's been under a lot of strain, and I've not helped. I can be depended on from now on to take over some of her load. If you guys could point me in the direction of the master bedroom and then take care of this little issue, I'll talk to her about things." They were very eager to help, and just as he was opening the door to the bedroom with her at his side, the towels were cleaned from the hallway, and he'd bet nearly sorted to each bathroom. As soon as he pulled the door shut behind him, she moved across the room to the furthest wall.

"I didn't handle that very well." He laughed. She was— "Why does me admitting to you that I fucked up funny to you every time? Or do you get your jollies when you find out that I've fucked up again?"

"No. What I think is funny is that you are the only person in the world that admits freely that you've fucked up. And to me, ordering the wrong color towels? That's not anything that would be considered a fuck up. More like a…Like a fortuitist mistake. They'll be easier to sort like you said, and so much easier to order the next time. Why are you suddenly out of towels anyway?" She told him why she'd ordered towels. "Oh. You know, that makes good sense. Ordering new towels every four years would certainly keep them thirsty and new-looking. To be honest, I don't know that I've ever used a brand-new towel. Are they thirstier, you know, so that the water on your body is gone rather than having to scrub hard to make them absorb?"

"Thirstier? You know, I've never thought of that before but that's when I get it in my head that the house needs new towels. Sort of a reminder." She cocked her brow at him, and he found himself wanting to see her do that more often. It was sort of sexy. "I'm sure you didn't come here to talk to me about towels. Did I have an appointment with you or something?"

"No. We didn't have anything scheduled, no. But we could. A date of sort." He asked her if they could talk in here or if they needed to go to an office. He also had business things to talk about. "I called several of the camera places to get an estimate. I handed it all to…I didn't catch his name when I came in. But I gave them to him."

"We don't have to go to the office, but I was about to have lunch. Would you like to join us?" He asked who would be joining them as they made their way down the hallway. "Dad usually comes over and we have like a power lunch. It's to catch up on the day before and talk about business meeting. By doing it at lunch, which I love, by the way, we can still take care of things that need attention in the same day and not have to talk about it at dinner. No business at dinner unless it's important. It's usually just him and me for dinner, and I don't want to miss dinner with him if you don't mind."

"You mean if I were to move in here." She nodded. "Moving in with you, just moving in, is on my list as well. I have about a dozen things that I need...well, I really need to talk to you about. There are a few things that aren't all that important, but I think we need to clear them up. Lunch, if that's what I smell, is what we're having. I am thrilled to eat with you and your father."

As if he'd summoned him, Alan came into the kitchen with them as they were sitting around an old but well-loved table. After giving him a huge hug, he told him that he was glad to see him. Donald, the butler he was told, brought him the file he had and he was as ready to join in conversations as they both were. He noticed that both Brandy and Alan had a list to tick things off of, and he pulled his own out. Glad not to be embarrassed for being old school and not pulling out a computer. Donald brought in several boxes and laid them between him and Brandy, and she said they were for him.

"The larger box is for you and your brothers. They're cell phones. I know you can talk to just about anyone you wish without one, but this will help when a client needs to get in touch with you. I was also thinking that instead of having the pack reach out to you when they need you if they were to use the phone to do that, it might well save you some time. You could ignore them too if you're busy with something else. But that's entirely up to you." He said he liked that idea. "Like I said, it's only a suggestion. Also, being delivered to the ranch house are computers. I wouldn't have gone ahead and ordered them if I wasn't certain that the six of you have been sharing the same computer for the last eleven years. It's going to be better if you all can work independently instead of waiting until your turn."

"Thank you. That actually knocked several things off of my list, too." She smiled at her dad, and he laughed. "Something wrong?"

"No. She told me that you'd want to come to this century, and I thought you'd not want to spend the money." Lica laughed too and said he hadn't looked up how much computers cost but knew that they were expensive. However, he knew, too, that they did need them. "Good man. I love working with you and your family."

They talked about what was on each of their lists. There wasn't any kind of order to what they talked about, nor was any subject on all their lists taken care of. He was going to go with the middle bid on the cameras for the ranch, and he was told to order the cattle from Texas to increase the herd that he had now. He was actually excited about being a huge landowner and ranch owner.

Alan left at two, telling them that he had things to do for his wife. She didn't join them for this meal, but she was usually there when they had lunch. Most nights, too, they would come to dinner. He was told that when his brothers could make it, they'd really like to have them nightly for dinner, too. It sounded good to him. After her dad left, he waited to see what she'd bring up next. She had asked him to stay for a bit longer.

"Two things that I want to bring up to you. Your mother has been pestering the household. Nothing they can't handle, but she seems to think that since you've married into money, you can put some cash into her account. I asked what that meant, and it was things like toothpaste and essentials that she would need to have shipped to her, or she could get them out of the prison store. I hope that it's all right, but I told the attorney to not help her out in any way and to demand that the prison not allow her to call here again." He thanked her and told Brandy that was just what he would have done. "Thank you for that. She will have to get a job, which the prison warden thought was a good idea as well."

"Great." She got up and poured herself some more tea, and did the same for him. He didn't know why, but he thought that she was like that all the time, fending for herself even though she had a full staff to take care of her every whim. "I'd like to move in here."

Just like they'd been told to do so or something, every other person in the room left them there. He asked her if he'd said something wrong. Shaking her head, she asked him if they could go to the office. She had some things to go over with him, too.

As soon as they were in the office, she closed the door behind him. He had no idea why, but he felt the need to kiss her, taste her. Pulling her into his arms, she turned her head away from his kiss, and no matter what he did, she wouldn't allow him to kiss her. That pissed him off so much that he wanted to pound his fist into the wall beside her.

"Do you love me?" He said no, too fast, he realized when she ducked under his arm to walk across the room. She kept her back to him so he couldn't see her face. "You said that kissing was too intimate for you. That you didn't love me, so you said there would be no kissing."

Chapter 6

"I don't like Lica, Mom, but I have fallen in love with him." Debra asked her if she'd told him. "No. But I did ask him if he loved me. He told me no. In fact, it was as if he'd been thinking about it, and he said *no* really fast. I've fallen in love with him, and I don't even like him. What am I supposed to do with this? Especially with the fact that he does not love me."

"Honestly, I don't know." She'd been surprised that they'd not had sex yet. The way that Lica looked at Brandy made her embarrassed at how much he seemed to want her. "This is beyond my knowledge of anything having to do with love. I mean, I've spoken to other shifters that work for us, but they actually thought that any day you'd be announcing that you're breeding. What they call being pregnant."

"It's doubtful that we'll ever have children. I mean, he was all right with us having sex the one time to bond with each other, but the chances of me conceiving from that have to be so low that I just don't see it happening. I couldn't care less about the magic. I've not used what I have, so I don't even know how much I'll get or have when we do." Debra's heart hurt with the knowledge that she had gotten from Brandy about not having children. But to her, it was still early days yet. "We only speak when it has to do with business information when we need something. He's done so well in learning how to run the business with me. I spent the entire day with Ivan when he was out at the ranch the other day. He's almost ready to take his boards to be a veterinarian. I'm really proud — and I love them too, of the way that they've accepted me and have made me feel welcome."

"Of course, they would do that. They're all good men, and I don't think that there is a bad egg in the lot of them." She thought about Lica. "Lica is odd, I'll say that. But I'd never believe it if you didn't tell me that he is so stubborn about things.

When he's around us, he is never anything but polite. But to hear this about him? I'm not so sure that I even like him all that much now."

"You aren't to hold this against him, Mom. I'm the one that put up such a fuss about sex with him." Debra asked if she regretted it now. "With all that I am."

Debra made her way home after making plans with Brandy later in the week. They'd talk more about Lica and her non-relationship with him, she was sure. But what could she do to help both of them along in this? Nothing. She could talk to Lica about Brandy loving him, but she'd made a promise that she would not. Unless he brought it up with her. Smiling, she thought of something else she could talk to him about. And made her way to the ranch where she knew he was working today.

He was shirtless coming out of the barn when she got there. He seemed really upset, and she wondered if this was a good idea to do today. As soon as he saw her, he told her he'd be back, and he ran back into the barn. When he came out, he was pulling his shirt back on. Lica was a nice piece of eye candy, she thought, then laughed.

"What do you know about the banker in town?" After asking for pleasantries, he dove right into what was bothering him. "For some reason, he's got it in his head that...are you busy? I would love for you to come with me when I go there to find out why he canceled my order for my cattle. I have a feeling that it's because I'm a 'damned upstart,' what he told my brother when he went to take money out of his account."

"My goodness. He actually canceled an order that had nothing to...Brandy told me that she gave you access to all the money she has, so I know for a fact that there is plenty of money in the accounts." Lica asked if she was all right with Brandy doing that. "Why would I care? It's her money anyway. And you're her husband, aren't you? There is no—never mind. Yes, Lica, I'd love to go with you to find out how this man thinks he can mess with my family."

While Lica was showering and changing his clothing, Debra called her daughter to let her know what was going on. Also that one of the other brothers wasn't able to get any money out of his account as well.

"You said you were going to the bank with

Lica?" She said she was. "Good. Don't mention it to anyone who put the money in the accounts. Nor that, if he doesn't know already that Lica and I are married. I'm sick of this man and his treating all shifters like they're not worthy of a bank loan."

"My goodness, I didn't know that this has been going on for a while. Yes, I'll not say a word. I'll even let Lica know that you're going to be taking care of things." She told her that he'd more than likely be upset about her interfering, but she wants that Slaven out. "You'll be fine, my dear. Let me know if you need anything from me."

After telling Lica what Brandy said she was going to do, he didn't react either way. As soon as they pulled up in front of the bank, he turned off the engine and looked at her.

"If I tell you to hide or get out of my way, you'll do that, won't you? I'd never forgive myself if anything were to happen to you." She patted him on the cheek and told him that she'd follow him to the ends of the earth if he'd give her a grandbaby. That was part of her things to talk about to him. "I don't know about that, Ms. Debra. We're still working things out between us. I think I messed up yesterday when I spoke to her about something."

"You mean when she asked you if you loved her? She loves you, did you know that, didn't you?" Oops. That did really just slip out and she hoped that Brandy could forgive her. Lica told her that she didn't like him, so there was no way that she'd love him. "Brandy told me that as well. She said that she didn't care for you overly much, but she had fallen in love with you. It broke my heart to see her — we should be getting to the bank before they close up."

He seemed like he was slightly shell-shocked to hear about Brandy loving him. But when she got out of his truck, one that she knew he'd picked out and bought the other day, she could tell that he had more questions. She was glad, too. Perhaps he'd think about how much her daughter had done for them and think a little more kindly of her. The truck that they all shared when they had to have something to get around in was about on its last legs. They were going to need everything more dependable from now on.

Opening the door, she could see Guy, one of Lica's brothers, at the cashier window at the end of the long line of about ten windows. Apparently, so did Lica, and he headed in that direction. Hanging back but not too far, where she wasn't able to hear what was going on, she saw Howard Slaven taking his short fat ass over to the window, where it was getting louder by the second. Pulling out her phone, she started recording the corner where things were going on.

"Why did you cancel my order? The one coming from Texas?" Slaven didn't look as if he had it in his head as to what Lica was talking about when he spoke. "You also might want to tell me why you're not allowing my brothers access to their accounts. It is their money, you know that, right?"

"I canceled the order because there isn't any way that you're going to be able to take care of those cows. Not to mention, how the hell were you going to afford them. Did you know that that order was for half a million dollars? You idiot, that's nothing that you could afford, or did you expect this bank to pick up the tab on what you did. That's not going to happen, young man. Not on my watch. In addition to that, what is the town going to do when you get tired of taking care of them, and they start to die off? You're lazy. All of your family is." Lica told the man that it was none of his business. "Of course, it is you moron. I'm the manager here, and I will guard this bank from people like you for the rest of my employment. And I'll allow them to get into their accounts when they tell me what they think they're doing if I allow them to take out that much money in one day. None of them have a job. Not even you. If you want to get more cows, then save up your money and buy them one at a time. That way, I can gauge how well you're going to do with them."

Debra didn't know what was going on when her husband and Brandy came into the bank and went up to two of the open windows where cashiers were standing. The cashier must have asked Brandy to hang on a moment, and then she left to talk to Slaven. Since she could hear better at the end where the banker was, she was able to hear that Brandy, Mrs. Fraizer, the girl called her, wanted to close her account.

Keeping an eye on her family, Debra stayed where she was recording the events unfolding. If shit were going to hit the fan, she wanted proof of what was being said and done. Having no idea what was going on, she had an inkling that Brandy and her dad were working on destroying the bank here.

While recording the people, she noticed that the other four brothers were doing the same. Going up to the open business windows and talking to the cashiers. She had an idea that this was planned by someone in the Frazier family and wondered if — then their grannie showed up and waited in line with her grandsons to do some banking. Debra just loved how Brogan would hug her grandsons while in public.

The little girl, well, she was an adult who had left Brandy at her window and waited on Slaven to answer her question. He didn't seem impressed when she repeated that Mrs. Fraizer wanted to withdraw all her money from her account and close it out. That was when Slaven laughed.

"I don't care if all the Fraziers want to empty their accounts. If they do, then more power to them. It'll be one less thing that I have to worry about daily. Yes, empty them if they want. It's not like it's going to hurt us if they do." He turned back to Lica and his brother. "Why don't you join your family, Lica, and empty out all your accounts. The clientele around here will certainly improve."

"Good idea." Brandy and her father were

finished up and on their way to the bank vaults when Slaven made his way to his office. The cashiers, all five of them, were laughing as they emptied one account for them after another. As soon as they had gotten the accounts closed out, the Fraizers would hug their brothers and head out of the building. When Lica, the last of the Frazier brothers, was at one of the windows, he turned to look in her direction. Since she'd been around all the Fraziers, her hearing had improved a great deal. But it mattered little. He spoke to her using their link, and she smiled when she didn't jump a foot off the ground.

"We're having dinner after I'm finished here, Ms. Debra. Your husband says that, at times, it startles the two of you when spoken to like this. Is this better?" He was so calm that she had to smile at him. She told him that she'd really like that. *"We're emptying our accounts as did your husband and Brandy. When he figures out what he's done, I don't think he's going to be employed much longer. Thank you for recording this. I have a feeling that the cameras aren't running here in the bank on the off chance that we, shifters, all of us, came in to sully his bank."*

Debra was still laughing as she walked out of

the bank with Lica. He was in a much better mood than he'd been before, and she was excited to see which one of them, Brandy or Lica, had come up with this plan. It was epic.

As soon as they were all out on the sidewalk after hugs were given to everyone, including from Lica to Brandy, they headed to the pizza place across the street. This way, they'd have front-row seats for whatever else Brandy had planned. As she'd said, this was her plan but it wasn't over just yet.

Just as they were finished giving their order for the table to share ten pizzas — she didn't know that it was going to be enough — police cruisers pulled up, as well as two vans with nothing on them to indicate who they were. Brandy told her that they were feds. They came to find out why several million dollars had been removed in one day at their bank.

"The bank can only hold two hundred fifty thousand for each person that has money in the bank. That's because two hundred fifty thousand is the limit for standard deposit insurance coverage per depositor, per FDIC-insured bank, and per ownership category will cover in the event of a robbery. With the five of you emptying your accounts, myself emptying four accounts, Dad and Mom emptying not just their business account but their personal one, leaving just Lica's in the back. When he closed out his own account and his new business account, that is a total of sixteen accounts that have the required maximum in them. Four million dollars removed from a single bank in a single day is going to make someone pay attention. And once those people start making calls—" Debra laughed when her cell phone, as well as Brandy's and her husband's, rang. No name showed up, but it did say Private Number. Then the one in front of Lica rang. "Don't answer them. I told Collett, the woman who helped me pull the wool over Slaven's eyes, to let them know we were having lunch across the street." Lica asked what she'd had Collett do. "She made sure to only say that Mrs. Fraizer was emptying her account. No first name. I don't know what she would have done had he asked, but he didn't. I was counting on him being excited about having the Fraziers out of his hair. What a dumb ass."

~*~

Lica would admit that he was having so much fun

that he didn't want to miss a second of it. But he still had to laugh when the Feds, as well as Slaven, joined them in the restaurant. Slaven was going on about how he wished Brandy had come to him personally about emptying out her accounts. He also told her several times that he'd take the money back, put it back into the accounts, and not worry about it. Brandy told him that she wasn't worried about a thing.

"Well, you've gotten me into a bit of a pickle with my boss, you see. You didn't allow me a little bit of a warning when—why don't we go back to my office, and we can talk about this. Your mother and father have done the same. I'd hate to have to call someone on you to get that money back—"

"Are you about to threaten my wife?" He wouldn't have said a word as Brandy seemed to have it under control, but Alan kicked him a little hard under the table and pointed to his wedding ring. Then he said make sure that everyone understood that Brandy was now Brandy Frazier. "It sounded to me like you were going to say something threatening. Because I was standing right there next to you when you said to let the Fraziers empty their accounts. I can tell you word for word what you said to Collett Mays when she asked you if Mrs. Fraizer wanted to close her account. You said, 'I don't care if all the Fraziers want to empty their accounts. If they do, then more power to them. It'll be one less thing that I have to worry about daily. Yes, empty them if they want. It's not like it's going to hurt us if they do.' Then you did this little gig thing and told me to go and empty my account. Remember? You said, and I quote, 'Why don't you join your family, Lica, and empty out all your accounts. The clientele around here will certainly improve.'"

"I did not say that. And if you could prove it, which is doubtful, too, how would I have known that Ms. Conner would lower herself to marry any one of you Fraizer men? Good Christ, you should go to the prison and move in with your mother."

Lica didn't know what possessed him, but he let just enough of his wolf go to scare, he supposed, the banker. Just as he was standing up to knock the ever-loving shit out of the man, he just disappeared. Like someone had come, picked him up and took off with him. Then he looked at Brandy. She was shaking her hand like a prize fighter would that had just KO 'ed someone in a ring.

"I could have been all right with him talking about me having to lower myself to marry you. I mean, so long as that piece of shit is lower than we are. But when he suggested that we move in with your mother?" Brandy shivered like it was too much to think about them living with their mom. "Well, it was just too ugly to think about. So I hit him. I think, however, I might have broken my finger. It hurts badly."

She put her hand out so that her dad could see it. But Lica pulled it to his mouth and kissed the red place on her hand, which was just beginning to turn purple. Looking up at her when he heard her sharp intake of breath, the lust in her eyes made him have to adjust not just his cock but his entire body before she pulled away and sat down again.

Lica missed a great deal while his mind and body were trying to think. About anything. Since all the blood in his body had gone to more private areas, he had nothing left to think with.

His family was all still talking—about what he didn't know. The police called an ambulance. He only knew that because when he'd been asked to move—Slaven had landed under the table when

Brandy slugged him, his brother told him that the police had made the call. He finally thought that he should have taken better care to look nice when the police started talking to him about the bank. And telling him how this was going to hit every newspaper in the country in the morning. But again, he didn't know what they were talking about. Not until he felt the sting of something hitting his cheek, then he looked at Brandy.

"What is wrong with you?" He told her that he didn't know. "Well, figure it out before I have to knock you around more. The police and the Feds have been trying to talk to you for the last twenty minutes. All you've done is—"

He stood up, jerking her into his arms, and kissed Brandy. He wanted to allow her to enjoy his kiss, but he was also afraid that if he let her go, even an inch, she'd pull away and hit him again. When she wrapped her arms around his shoulder and then his neck, he had to admit that he was still slightly afraid of her. But when she opened for him, giving him the taste of her that he wanted all along, he pulled her tighter to his body and deepened the kiss.

"Lica." He growled at the brother, who was

pulling on his shoulder. "Come on, Lica. You're embarrassing everyone. Lica, you have to stop before you go too far." He lifted his head and looked into the lust-glazed eyes of Brandy before speaking.

"I'm in love with you, Brandy. I think I have for a long time." His brother, Ayden, told him that everyone knew that, but the Feds were asking him questions. "I don't care. All of you, go away."

It was the gun that seemed to be trying to enter his forehead that finally had him letting go of Brandy. When she was jerked back from him, Lica growled, but it was Edmond who took care of the FBI agent who touched her. He shifted to his wolf so quickly that he didn't see it coming. He knocked the man from Brandy and set himself on his chest with his paw digging deeply into his chest. He was sure that the wolf's mouth around his throat was keeping him from speaking right then.

"Wolves, especially alphas, are very possessive of their mates. I'd remember that next time if I were you. He could have ripped your throat out, and no one would have harmed him for protecting his alpha bitch." The officer with the feds said that he'd kill him if he tried that with him. This time, it was Guy who shifted. The officer was flat on his back with a paw in his chest before he could touch his gun. Then, when Guy moved his mouth around his throat, the man whimpered. "Are you so sure about that?"

"Okay, you have the bigger balls, Mr. Fraizer. If you promise not to hurt any more of my men, I'd like to get this cleared up. Mr. Slaven is saying that you made Mrs. Frazier take her money out of his bank." He laughed a little. "I don't even want to think about how that's even possible. Your wife strikes me as a woman who does what she wants when she wants. She's smart too."

"Thank you. I'm beginning to see that for myself. And yes, I promise that I won't harm your men so long as they remember that I belong to her, and I will do anything to protect her. Anything." The man nodded, and then Lica looked at Brandy before answering the question. "Sir, as you've guessed, I have never been more proud of my wife and family for what transpired today than at any other time in their lives. Mr. Slaven has been a tyrant for the last twenty years, and you can ask any shifter in this town about that."

Since they were all in a public place, crowded

now with others who had come to see what was going on, the shifters started talking about how Slaven had kept them from getting a home loan. That he'd gotten them fired from their jobs when they were to go to the doctor, and Slaven wouldn't allow them to withdraw money to see the doctor. So, no note, and that would cause them to lose their jobs.

There were other horror stories like that. Mr. Caraway had had to bury his wife when Slaven had denied him a loan that would have given her a nurse to be with her during the day. It was Alan who told about how Slaven had canceled the check and order for the cattle that Lica had ordered.

"It would have employed fifty more people in the town. Not to mention, it brought in revenue when we started building the slaughterhouse, which would employ more people." Slaven said it was all lies, that all the Fraziers were a lazy lot. "Really? You have proof of this? Because I've been a businessman for all my life and these men are worthy. Men of worth, I have to tell you, isn't something that you see all the time. Hell, had my daughter not been his wife, I think I might well adopt him as my son. All of them." Alan smiled at him. "Can you imagine the kids these two will have? Hell, all of them having children will make this town and world a better place just because they're in it."

"Thank you." Alan hugged him and told him that he was serious about adopting him. "But for now, I'm going to have a lot of making up to do to your daughter."

Lica felt his eyes fill with tears when Brandy took his much larger hand into her tiny one. He, after locking his fingers through hers, kissed the back of her hand and paid attention to what was going on around him. He had a mate, a good one, and he really did have a lot of making up to do. The most important thing was he needed to tell her how profoundly sorry he was for every time he'd hurt her. And he knew that he had.

Howard Slaven was arrested. The list of crimes that he'd committed against the shifters — prejudicial treatment on not just loans but canceling checks, denying access, as well as a plethora of other things was going to see him in prison for a very long time. The very fact that he had canceled a half-million dollar check that was paying for goods that were shipped out already was going to be under the mail fraud law, he'd heard. Christ, he was never so happy to see someone get into trouble than he was that bastard.

By the time the bank was closed down, it would more than likely be that way for a few months. Arrangements were made for people to get money if they needed it. It was well after ten o'clock at night. He was exhausted but exhilarated as well. The family made their way to their homes, and he realized that his brothers were still living in the ranch house. It was crowded when he lived there with them, and he couldn't believe that he'd not thought of them getting a house. More than likely, they would have been turned down, was his next thought.

"I almost forgot. I heard from the attorney group that was with Green. He's been arrested, I didn't ask why, but he's currently in jail. The company that his daughter took over is doing very well. I did go ahead and lend her the money, I should have told you that, but she isn't going to expand right away. I suggested that she needed to use the extra money to make her employees, all of them, feel like they're a part of something that is going places. She wants to get things back on the correct track, meaning her employees are all right with coming to work knowing that their benefits are being taken care of. She asked for ideas on how to make them feel like they're all a team by start treating her employees to a lunch once in a while. Also, to hand out gift cards when she sees one of them doing something well. I have that kind of thing going on around a few of my businesses. Also, when she can afford it, I told her that she needs to figure out a way to close up during the holidays for two weeks for Christmas and pay her people."

"When I worked for Mr. Wilkins, he would work Christmas alone so that his men could have the day off. If he got into trouble, anyone of them would have come in to help. Also, while he worked the entire night before and the day of Christmas, his men would come in and spell him a bit so that he could go have his meals. When he passed away, everyone in town had a good story to tell about the Wilkins. They had a lot to do with us being the men that we are today." She said that was a nice story. That she was also sure that people would say the same about him and his brothers. "I hope so. But it's your view of me that is concerning me the most."

"I love you." His breath caught when she smiled at him after declaring her love for him. He stood there, trying to form words around the lump in his throat, when he decided that he needed to just say what he was thinking all along about her.

"I love you as well, Brandy Fraizer. I think I have since I met you, but I was just too...not stubborn but jaded to see that I could have a wonderful life with you if I just got my head out of my ass." She agreed with him, which made him laugh. "Are you forever going to be telling me the truth, no matter what it's about?"

"Yes. You can count on that." They were both exhausted but he did ask her if she'd sleep in the big bed with him. She said that she was too tired to walk down the hall and went to the bathroom to change, she said. While she was getting ready for bed, Lica got under the covers. He thought that he'd wait for her to come to bed but was out before she got out of the bathroom.

Chapter 7

Brandy woke wrapped around Lica. She'd heard that shifters run hotter than humans, but he was lying next to a furnace. For being a wolf, it surprised her that he wasn't covered in hair. Not even his arms were overly hairy like she imagined that one would be.

Lica was still sleeping soundly and quietly, so she took the opportunity to look at his face. It was a handsome face, she had always thought so, but it was hard, too. Like he was a working man. She wanted to make it so that he could be a man of leisure and not work so hard daily to make ends meet. But then she dismissed that thought when she realized that he'd be bored. Not to mention upset that she'd expect him to be inside lounging around the house every day. Brandy knew that she would be if she were to be just a housewife.

When he opened one eye and looked at her, his smile made her heart skip several beats in her chest. She would only tell him this if he asked, but she thought since she'd fallen in love with him, he was the only reason that her heart beat at all. That she was able to breathe. The reason that air moved in and out of her lungs. Lica asked her if she'd been awake long, and she shook her head as he moved to his back, pulling her to him so that her head was across his chest.

"No. Not long at all. I'm usually up by five-thirty most mornings anyway so that I can get most of any housework done that needs to be tidied up. Also, if I have a meeting first thing, I'll be able to refresh my memory on things that I want to talk about. When are you up? I'm assuming that sleeping in to you is not a common thing." He told her that he was usually up by dawn, he needed to get his chores done for the cattle. "I can see that. I'm thinking that, like you, they're used to having you out there with them early, too. Is it true that you don't eat breakfast until after you milk the cows?" She was serious but the look on Lica's face had her laughing.

"Yes. But since I've been expanding the herd, I've hired a few people to come in and get the milkers set up for them. So I can have a bit of meat when I get up, and I won't expire too soon." He laughed. "Yes, I have breakfast before I go to the barn to start working. Sheesh woman. Also, I don't have many breeding cattle right now. Did I tell you that the Feds took care that the herd that Slaven cancelled is still going to come to me? Thank goodness for that. They're even picking up the tab for what we did to help them with Slaven." She told him that was wonderful. "It is. Since meeting you, I've never had so many things coming my way. Thanks to you."

"I didn't do anything but believe in you. Which wasn't hard. You already had..." She felt stupid when she said that and told him that. "I meant that all I did was provide you with the funds that—that's not right either. I'm going to be quiet now before I say something completely stupid, and I have to leave the house before I get a shower." He laughed with her.

"I want you. I won't even try and deny how much I want you. Even before I figured out what a dumbass I am, I still wanted you. But I have a meeting today at noon, and it's important that I'm on time. It's some…you know what? You should come with me. I'd love that. There are several hundred acres of land that is up for sale, and I've been asked to see it before it goes to market. I've been using the same realtor since we bought the first bit of land at the auction. She's never steered me wrong, and I trust her to disclose everything about the property, too." She asked him if it was the Apple Farm. "Yes. You've already purchased it, haven't you?"

"No. Dad was thinking of buying it if he came to market. But I don't think he ever expected it to hit the market in his lifetime. The son, he's about my age and will more than likely get it when they're finished with the background checks on who else might be out there. From what I heard, his parents didn't have a will. My mom has fallen in love with the cabin that is set up in the woods behind the main house. It was put there by the couple to live near their son when he was able to move in. But the parents died. I've not been keeping up with everything, so I might well have missed a great deal. I've never seen the house nor the cabin, but Mom has been wanting it since Mr. Apple and his wife died. I wonder why it took so long to come to market." Lica told her what he'd been told. "I hear about that sort of thing happening all the time with elderly people, them not having a will. But their son dying? I didn't know anything about that. And he didn't have a will either? How sad. Not having a will or anyone to leave their things to ends up being in probate for years." He asked if she had one. "I do. It's not been updated since I met you, so I guess we'll have to get on that. My parents have theirs all made out, I think. But to see the house and land? Yes, I would love to go with you. Would you mind if Mom and Dad were to come with us?"

"No, I don't mind at all if they were to come with us. I love your parents. They're wonderful people." She agreed with him. "They did a great job in raising you too. You're brilliant."

"You don't need to butter me up, Lica. I'm going to have sex with you." He got up laughing. Telling her that he was going to take a shower, she got up herself. Moving around the layout of the bedroom always irritated her. The whole house seemed to be laid out oddly. Walls that were just there. Also, and this bothered her more than anything, none of the windows matched. Even if they were in the same room. Some would be short, some tall. There was one room where it looked as if the windows had been put in sideways. It was then that it occurred to her that she didn't like this house. And she hadn't since she'd seen it the first time. But it was close to her parents' home then when she needed a place to live. There was something so sad about how it seemed to tell her that the previous owners hadn't enjoyed it either.

Thinking about the windows, she decided to call someone to have all the windows replaced while it was still warm enough to get it done. Then, she was going to have all the carpets pulled up. They were about twice the age of her and she hated carpeting in the bedrooms. She put that on her list of things to do today. She went into the bathroom while Lica was showering.

"Would you like to live in the big house there if the house is livable? I just decided that I don't want to live here. I'm going to have the windows replaced before we sell it as well as the carpets taken up. This house needs to be cleaned up and made to balance. I want to start a new life with you, and this house isn't going to be good for us." He asked her how long that would take. "I don't know, to be honest. But if it seems like it's taking too long, we'll hire more people to make it happen faster."

"I know that the other house has been sitting empty for a while. It might be just too old to do much with. What would you do with this house?" She told him that one of his brothers could have it if they wanted it. "Edmond loves this house. He did mention that he didn't care for the windows being all whopper-jawed, but I can see him living here."

"Good. We'll take care of that when we figure out what to do with the land. If the house isn't worth the effort of cleaning it up, then we'll build. That will take longer, but it'll be more in line with what we're wanting." She put that on her list, too. She loved lists. "We're going to need to hire a full staff. With both of us working, a house of any size will get out of hand in no time."

When he turned the water off, she stepped out of the bathroom. They were really running behind, and she was sure that if she saw him in all his glory, they'd never leave the house. He was laughing when he came out of the bathroom with a towel, not nearly big enough to wrap around his waist, when she entered the bathroom to get her shower. Brandy screamed when he opened the shower door and joined her in the large stall.

"We're just going to be late, I'm afraid." She wrapped her arms around his shoulders as he pressed her against the wall. "Christ, I love you.

Lica bit her lip, and she nearly came. As his teeth sank into her lips so hard that she cried out with it. When he dropped to his knees in front of her, she knew that she was going to come soon and she couldn't wait. Brandy was so wet she was embarrassed by it. Not even the shower was enough to cover up how it seemed to flow from her body.

"I need to taste you, Brandy. I want to see if you taste as wonderful as you smell." He pulled her to him by way of grabbing her ass. She cried out again when he nipped at her thigh. "Sit down on the shower seat, love. I want to feel you come down my throat."

Her body was responding before her mind could come up with a reason why this was a bad idea to be having this kind of sex in the shower.

Lica was between her legs, which he'd put on either side of his head before she could protest if she was ever going to. As soon as he pulled her clit into his mouth, she cried out his name and came. Never had anything made her feel this way.

He ate her like he was never going to stop. The more he took from her, the more he gave her, the more she wanted. Every time he bit down on her clit, she came crying out his name. Every time he slid his tongue into her sheath, she knew she was soaking him. When he slid his fingers into her, she rode his hand, her hips coming up off the seat like he was fucking her. It was then that she realized that she wanted him to make her scream while he was deep inside of her.

"Come for me again. Come and let me drink from you again." She leaned back, her body so taunt with need that when he sucked her clit into his mouth as he stretched her with his fingers, she bowed up off the seat and begged for him to slow down in one breath and to make her come quickly in the next. He never stopped taking her, even when he begged him to stop.

When he stood up over her, she could see that his cock looked painfully full. The thought of him taking her, his thick cock entering her, she knew that it was going to hurt. But instead of sliding into her like they both wanted, he fisted his cock until long streams of his precum fell onto her. Not even the warmth spraying over the two of them could wash it away. It was coming so fast.

"I wasn't going to take you the first time against the wall here in the stall. I thought about the bed, but it's simply too far away." He moaned when she reached for him. "Honey, you touch me, and it's going to be over right now. I want to come all over you. Have my cum spray all over your pretty pussy until you come again. Tell me you want it. Tell me, Brandy, tell me you want me."

"Please." He leaned over her and took her mouth. She could feel the head of his cock just at her breasts. When he bowed back, lifting his head from her, he roared out as he came all over her. The heat of it felt wonderful. Each time it touched her in a different place, she would rub it into her flesh. Her nipples got the most of his cum, and she licked her fingers as she took some of it to her mouth. His loud growl had her nearly coming again.

Suddenly she was jerked from the seat, his body pressing her against the wall, and his cock slammed into her until she screamed with the pain and pleasure of it. He was so thick, stretching her to the limit of her pussy. Nothing could have prepared her for such wonderful enjoyment, and she could have died right then—as happy as anyone could—because of the way he was giving her his all.

Over and over, he took her hard, his mouth nipping at her flesh, soothing the skin when he hurt her, and she loved it. His cock slid in and out, bringing her such joy with the shape and size of his cock. Teeth so sharp drew little wounds all over her that she didn't care about at all. Pain and pleasure so wonderfully amazing, she never wanted him to stop. When he told her to come, he commanded her, and she did so like it was the most natural thing to do. To come screaming by a man plowing her like he was an animal that she knew he could be.

Lica held her to his body while he fucked her slowly. His cock was still inside of her, and she was afraid to move. Not afraid, just…she didn't want this to end, for him to pull away from her and leave her. She wanted more from him but was afraid that she'd make him come too soon and she'd not get to come like that again.

She had no idea if she could arouse him again by moving so that he'd want her again so she stood very still. This, this sex with him, was nothing like she'd ever had before. No man had made her feel the things that she did with Lica.

Even after sex, she was never satisfied as she is now, even if she'd come fifty times while having — it occurred to her why it was so different then. That had been sex, this, even as violent and quick as it had been, was making love with someone that she loved. That was the difference. When he lifted his head and looked down at her, she smiled at him and asked him if he was all right. She told him she'd never been better.

"I think I hurt you. No, I know that I did, and I'm so sorry. Please tell me that you forgive me." She told him she was ready for another romp when he laughed. "Brandy, look at me so I can see how badly I hurt you. I was too rough on you, I think."

"You didn't hurt me at all. I mean, just a little. I've had sex before, but not with anyone as big as you are." Her face heated up, and she reached over and turned off the shower spray. "I'm such a dunce. I very much enjoyed that." She glanced at the clock and reminded him that they had to get going. "But I want to have sex in our bed soon."

"That's a promise I can keep for you." When he handed her one of the towels he'd gotten out of the linen closet in the bathroom, she told him some of the things she didn't like about this house. It was a way to distract herself from the pain of moving around. It made her grin when she noticed that he was moving slowly like she was. It was good for her heart and mind to know that she had given him some twinges, too.

They barely beat her parents to the house. The realtor was there, of course but she didn't mention that she'd been waiting very long. While they were going over the specs of the land, Brandy waited on Lica so they could tour the house together. Her parents were walking around the lower level of the three-story house while she listened to what needed to be repaired as soon as possible, like the roof and what could be held off.

"The entire house was upgraded last year. I also learned that he had water lines put out in the fields to water the horses that he was planning on breeding. The son, James, did that before the will couldn't be found. Since he figured that he was going to get the house, he made a great many improvements to the place to get it ready to be moved into. That didn't end up working out for him in the long run, I'm sad to say." Lica asked Lonnie, the realtor, what had happened. "He was killed in an auto accident about four months ago. By then, the house was in disarray from the projects and had to be finished or the house would need to be torn down. He didn't have a will either. People really need to get over the idea that they're going to live forever and not bother with one. Anyway, he didn't have any family, so after the hearing about the house going to him since his parents were both gone, they had to have another hearing about what to do with the house again. It was determined that the house needed to sell and soon so that all the money that he'd poured into the house wouldn't be for naught. There isn't any family left of the Apples so it was sell it or let it go to ruin. I love that someday another family can make it work out for them."

After the realtor left them, she had to pick up her son from school as he was ill. She and Lica started at the top of the house, finding out that it had a fourth floor that looked like a playroom for children. Her parents joined them.

Her mom and dad were in love with the cabin as she had told Lica and said that if they bought the house, they'd pay half of the loan in order to live on the land in the cabin. He looked at her as he told them what he wanted to see happen. "How about you guys be babysitters when we have kids and not pay us anything to be close to us when we need help or advice. I'm really going to need some help on being a good parent to any children that we have. You guys are the best role models that I could have asked for." Brandy loved that idea and told him so. "I was hoping you'd say that. You're breeding—you're pregnant now. I can tell because...well, just because."

The hugs were amazing. Brandy was afraid. She'd have to admit that. Their love was so new to the two of them that she didn't want to end up being a single mom if he decided that he didn't love her. But when he put his hand on her flat tummy and told her how much he loved them both, she kissed him, thanking him for being such a wonderful person. Now anyway, she said with a laugh.

"We'll need to make an offer and see where that leads us. I don't think she ever mentioned the price of the house. Is there anything on the paperwork?" Dad found flyers in the kitchen on the counter. There wasn't a price but a phone number for Lonnie. Calling and having to leave a message, they decided to go to her parent's home and have dinner. Steaks on the grill sounded great, and Brandy couldn't wait to go home and get her body fucked again.

~*~

Brandy had just come out of the bathroom when Lica knocked lightly on the bedroom door. Hearing from Lonnie about the price of the Apple house was good news, but she had her real estate attorney call with a counteroffer. Within a few minutes, no more than ten, they were told that the house and all the land were theirs for the purchase price they'd agreed on. Dad pulled out the champagne that he'd been saving, and there were full glasses all the way around.

Looking down at herself, she wondered what she'd been thinking when she had bought the tiny little nightie that she had on. It was a beautiful shade of blue, her favorite color and there were little strings at the shoulders and her hips that held it on her.

"I got this a few days ago. I don't know then what I was thinking but it such a delicate thing, don't you think?" He didn't move. Didn't say a word as she felt the need to explain why she was wearing it. "I should have gotten something more practical, I guess."

Lica stood in the doorway staring at her for so long that she wondered if he was upset. When he took off his jacket and tossed it in the general direction of the chair, she watched him move across the room toward her as he undressed.

"You bought this the other day?" She nodded and ran her fingers over the small squares of silk that just barely covered her breasts. "I hope you didn't pay too much for it because it's going to be nothing but a rag when I'm finished with you."

"You aren't going to get to take it off me. I'm going to take it off me for you." He nodded and licked his lips as he stood within touching distance of her. "I'm going to strip you down as well. How would you like that?"

He stretched his neck, and she heard it pop. She would never have believed it, but it was about the sexiest thing she'd ever heard. Then he smiled. Though, it didn't remind her of a smile so much as it looked like a predator that had just found his prey.

"Slow and easy, baby. Do it to me, slow and easy." She walked her fingers up his chest to his chin, then kissed him. Hearing him moan, it made her wet and needy. "Do you have any idea how sexy you look right now? Turn for me. Little by little, please. I need to see the entire thing so that I can think about you dressed like this when I'm all alone out in the fields."

She turned slowly and then looked at him over her shoulder. She liked the way he was staring at her, and she winked at him as she turned and moved behind him.

"I'm going to strip you down, then I'm going to taste all of you. Starting with your cock." He groaned, and she rubbed her hand over his thick cock. "Maybe we won't get much further than that as hard as you are."

"Are you going to take me into your mouth, Brandy?" She nodded and dropped to her knees in front of him. "Then we won't get much further than that. Because the movement I slide down the back of your throat, I'm going to come. The thought of you...Christ, you look good enough to eat right now."

"I love it when you eat me. I come so hard just knowing that you're drinking my juices." She squealed when she was suddenly air-born. He had picked her up and tossed her on the bed so fast that she bounced twice before she landed in the middle. He was on her before she could guess what he was going to do.

"I told you I was close." His hands slid up her thighs and under the tiny little strings at the sides of her panties. "You're going to have to suck me some other time. Right now, I need to lap at your pussy until you come down my throat, then I'm going to fuck you from behind until you scream out my name."

He didn't waste any time as he buried his face between her legs. She screamed when he nipped at her clit and came hard and fast. He was lapping at her before she could catch her breath and came twice more before he lifted his head and looked at her.

"I want to fuck you like this." She nodded as he moved up her body, putting her legs on his shoulders. "It's going to be deep and hard. I want you to come as many times as you can as you take me."

He entered her just as her hips came up off the bed. He had her nearly bent in half when he started pounding into her. She had never had him this deep before, and when he tore off her nightie, she reached up and took her nipples in her fingers and twisted them hard. Her climax took her so hard she nearly fainted from it. When he pulled his cock from her, she reached for him, but he pushed her away.

"On your knees. I need to pound into you like an animal." She moved to do his bidding but wasn't fast enough. He flipped her over and jerked her to his cock so fast that she cried out again.

He curled his body around her and fucked her in fast, hard strokes until she was dizzy from it. As soon as he cupped her breast, he licked along her shoulder, and she knew that he was going to bite her. She pressed back against him as she prepared her for his marking.

"When you come, I'm going to bite you. Hard. And when I do, I'm going to hurt you. The need to claim you is making my wolf crazy." She felt his teeth graze her shoulder. "Christ, I need you."

She screamed loud and long when he bit her. Brandy felt her shoulder crush under his bite and knew that his wolf was just as much a part of him as Lica was. When he pulled back, scaring her back with his teeth, Brandy felt his fingers dig deep into her hips and felt something inside of her snarl at her to let go when he did. As soon as Lica threw back his head and howled, his voice echoing around the room, Brandy did as well. Her entire body was alive with the climax that ripped from her. As she lay under him, breathing hard and feeling fucking fantastic, she wondered if it would always be like this for them. Lica chuckled and sealed the wound at her shoulder.

"You will always be my mate, and I will forever want to mark you. So, in answer to your thoughts, yes, it will always be like this between us."

"I'm glad. I don't know what I'd do without you." He told her he didn't want to find out what life would be without her and pulled her into his arms when he lay on the bed. "We're going to be late getting up in the morning, you know that, don't you. I think this is going to be a thing for us, being late for important matters. Signing off on the paperwork for the new property shouldn't have been scheduled so early. Edmond wants to go with us so that he'll know how it goes when he buys the house we're in. I didn't tell him that we were giving it to him. I'm going to have to remember that and not schedule meetings early anymore."

Laughing, she told him she didn't care and closed her eyes. "Edmond will have to find his own mate, and he'll understand." And she hoped that they all found their mates so they could all feel this wonderful all the time.

Chapter 8

David knew that if he didn't kill that fucking bitch he was going to die soon. Why she cut off his hand wasn't cool. She should have given him more warnings before doing what she did. He said as much to his brother Carl.

"She did warn you, David. She told you three times that she wasn't going to put up with you smart-mouthing her in her own home." He reached over and punched his brother in the face. "That ain't right. I was just telling you what you seem to forget every time you talk about making her pay. If you want my advice, I think—"

"I don't want your advice, you fucking turd." Carl just huffed at him and got up off the couch. The bloody lip that he'd given his brother was already healed. The mother fucker healed quickly every time he hit him. It wasn't right, damn it. He looked down at his wrist.

He'd been sitting with it in a bowl so that the blood wouldn't get all over the furniture. Every couple of hours, he'd shift to try and heal the wound that the cunt had given him, but all it did was open the wounds that he'd had sewn shut several times since his hand had been removed. Getting up and dumping the bowl on the couch, he was out the door before his mom could knock him around. That bitch needed to go too.

She'd agreed with the bitch about cutting his hand off. Mom told him that it wasn't right that he had disrespected the alpha in her own home. Not to mention, him going into the house like he had owned it. Mom said that she'd knocked him three ways from Sunday for doing that in her house. Again, he'd not asked her for her advice, but she seemed to have a great deal of it to share. Bitches, all of them.

Making his way out to his car, he was in it and down the driveway in minutes. He'd had to get him a newer car because his truck had caused him trouble due to his inability to shift with his hand all bloodied up. That was something else the bitch was going to pay for, him a new car.

David was just about to pull into the parking lot of the bar he'd been going to since he'd been bigger when he spotted the bitch and her mate out walking around. They were holding hands like they were in love or something. Christ, he was never going to fall in love. It made you look about half-sappy.

Pulling up on the curb right in front of them, the man, he didn't ever think that he'd call him his alpha shoved the bitch behind him. Like that was going to stop him from getting to her. He'd be taking him out, too. David puffed out his chest a little more when he realized that the fucker looked to be about twice his size. Then the bitch came out from behind the big man.

"You take it back." She told him no. Just like that, no. Like she had every right to tell him no, like he wasn't anything. "You heard me. I said to take it back. You had no right to do what you did to me."

"Really? Would you like for me to recount that day's events to remind you of your stupidity?" She was using words that he didn't understand. "I wanted to know if you wanted me to tell you what happened that day. Remind you that I more than once told you to behave yourself."

"I'm not a kid. You don't get the right to tell me to behave like I'm a baby." She just cocked her brow at him, and he looked at the fucker standing next to her when he laughed. "What the fuck do you find so funny? I'm standing here with no hand, and you're making me pissed off."

"First of all, I have a feeling that you're always pissed off. Secondly, I was laughing when I thought of the look on your face when my wife, and you'd be wise to remember that, cut your hand off in one blow. That, if you think about it takes a great deal of power. And she did it in one blow. I'm pretty proud of her. You should be, too. I think it would have been harder on you if she'd taken more than one chop at your wrist to remove it." He said she shouldn't have hurt him in the first place. "Really? I guess, in your small mind, she wasn't justified in making an example of you being an ass. In her own home, as she pointed out to you several times."

"I'm going to kill you both." The man seemed to just get bigger. Like he wasn't already big enough. The bitch laughed, and he looked over at her. Christ, she looked like she'd grown a foot in those few seconds. His bravo was leaving him a little at a time—bravo. A new word he'd heard and was trying to use it all the time now. However the couple didn't seem all that impressed with him. Then they went and turned their backs on him and started away. "Hey? I'm not done with you two yet. You get your asses back here. This ain't done yet."

"It was done the moment that my wife cut your hand off. You should learn your manners before someone teaches them to you." Bitch asked him if his momma was proud of him. He smiled at her. "I would imagine that she's sick of his whinnying, too. I know that I am, and I don't have to live with the little cock sucker."

He shifted and lunged at the couple. As soon as he landed on his sore paw, he knew a kind of pain that made him sick. Before he could touch either of them, the man slapped him in the nose. Nothing, not even getting your balls slapped hurt like having your nose smacked. Whimpering, he moved away from them so he'd not get hurt again as he growled at them.

"You're the biggest dumbass I've ever seen. Do you have any idea who I am? What I am to you?" Snarling again, he lifted his leg and pissed in the direction of the two of them. He wouldn't get close enough to be hurt again, but David prided himself on having a long-range piss. "I'm going to talk to your mother about you when you're dead. Because the moment you shifted in front of me, that was the end of your life. You fucking little shit."

"Shift." He felt himself turn inside out when the bitch told him to shift. "Shift. Shift. Shift." Each time she commanded him to do it, he could feel the pain coming off his wolf. When she finally stopped, he lay there as his wolf, with his body so abused that he couldn't move. When she knelt down in front of him, David didn't have the strength to swipe at her. Panting, his wolf curled around his body as if to say, shut the fuck up and go home, he snarled at her again.

"Would you like to feel that pain for the rest of your life, David? I don't have to be near you to make you do what I want. In fact, I'm planning on staying as far away from you as I can for the next—how long do you suppose he can live after what we did to him, Lica?" He said it was getting closer to it only being minutes. "Yes, I'll have to agree with you. He's losing a great deal of blood right now."

He was, too. Not just from his paw, but his nose was bleeding, too. And it would never stop bleeding until the man, the supposed alpha, forgave him. Christ, this was a nightmare. All he wanted to do was kill the two of them so that he'd have the alpha position.

This time, the man leaned down to speak to him. As much as he wanted to rip his throat out, David knew that he needed to rest a bit. His body was worn out. His heart seemed to be beating a tad too slow. Standing up, falling back over as soon as he did, he whimpered again before speaking to them.

"I'm going to allow the two of you to live for another day." They both laughed. He didn't blame them. He knew that he was a mess. "You won't think it's so funny when I slit your throats in the middle of the night soon. You're going to be dead as dead can be."

"Is there another form of dead that we don't know about?" The man stood up. "I don't have time for this bullshit. You apologize to my wife and myself, and I'll heal you. Otherwise, and you can bank on this, David James, I'm going to kill you where you lay. I don't want to have to keep looking over my shoulder for you. You're just stupid enough that you'd keep trying until I bore of you, and that will be the end of your entire family, too."

"Kill them all. Do you think that I care? My mother has been telling me that I'm stupid and dumb my entire life. I could care less if she took another breath." The bitch asked him if he was serious. "Yes. Christ, she's in my face about every little thing. I cannot wait to be able to piss on her grave for all the things that she'd done to me. Kill them all. I find that I would be better off without them."

He wasn't going to turn around and see what was behind him. Both the bitch and the man were looking over his shoulder like he was going to see. When he heard his mother telling the couple, there wasn't any way that she'd be talking to him about that sort of shit, about how he'd made her life hell since he'd been a little boy. That she despaired of him ever amounting to anything.

"I doubt that he'd going to be any help to me in my golden years either." She got down on her knees, and he thought for sure that this was going to be epic. His mother was going to beg for him to be alpha like he'd been planning and plotting for his entire life, but all she did was bare her throat to the couple. "I pledge myself to you, Alpha Lica Fraizer and Alpha Bitch, Brandy Fraizer. I will forever be a servant to you and my pack."

The moment that the man, he'd not known that his name was Lica, touched his mother, he turned to him. While he wasn't afraid of the man, he certainly made an impressive wolf. When the bitch shifted, something that she seemed to be happy about the way she was dancing around, she turned to look at him when she settled down. Lica smiled, his wolf making it look like he was all badassed or something.

"David Arthur James, I sentence you to death by pack." He looked over his shoulder, and David was suddenly terrified. "Take him. Kill him."

David felt his body lift up. Not like he was going to be able to stand picked up but like he was tossed into the air. And he was. Several times, from wolf to wolf, they tossed his body from one group to the next while working their way to the field behind the town. Each time he came down, he lost a bit more of himself. Fur was torn from his skin. His paws were torn away from him with no more than a snap of their teeth. But the time he was in the field, he didn't have the strength to bed. His mouth had been ripped open, and his gut was hanging out of his belly like some kind of odd art project covered in blood.

He didn't know one wolf from the next. While he could see enough to know where he was, there was something wrong with one of his eyes. Then it saw it hanging from the mouth of someone he thought was his brother. Christ, was no one going to take his side in anything? The alpha was watching the entire thing. And when David's throat was ripped out, he knew that he was as good as dead when he realized that his mother had killed him like he was nothing to her.

~*~

Ayden had been working at this place for the last several weeks. Brandy told him all he had to do was observe what was going on, but it wasn't easy to see much by just going into the place and having a meal. The food was all right, not great, and the service he was getting was a lot to be desired, but he couldn't figure out for the life of him why they were losing money.

The portion sizes weren't too big. It didn't look to him like much was coming back by way of dirty plates. However, last night's numbers indicated that they lost over seven thousand dollars. He wouldn't have guessed that they had served that much in the way of food.

"Hey, Andy," He corrected the night manager again that wasn't his name. "I don't care. Do you want your free meal or not? I'm going to be closing up soon. It's almost nine o'clock now."

Time, when he was busy, seemed to get away from him quickly. Telling Mr. Hobby that he would love something to eat, he took off his apron and made his way to the back of the restaurant. Being a busboy brought back all kinds of memories. Hardly any of those were good, but he was making decent money, he supposed. As soon as the thick steak was set in front of him, Ayden looked at the cook when he sat down across from him.

"I've been watching you, Frazier. I'm thinking that you're a man who could use some extra cash all the time. Am I right, or am I wrong about that?" Ayden simply told him that he thought everyone could use a bit extra at times. "Yeah, I thought so. I got us a thing going on here that nobody has figured out yet. You like playing poker?"

He hated card games. He was good at them, but he nodded that he did all right at it. After explaining the rules to him, although he was not sure where this was going, the manager came back and sat at the break table with them. There were two more people who joined them. One of them was the waitress that he'd met earlier. She wasn't anything but a pain in the ass and a bitch to boot.

"Okay, you got the rules?" Forgetting that he should be paying attention better, he simply said yes. Whatever was going to happen tonight, he had a feeling that it was going to be the explanation for how the restaurant was doing so poorly. "All right. The winner takes all. You got that? If you win, which I don't see how you will, you get to take out all the meat in the locker and sell it off. That's one part of the rules. Then you bring back the money that you made when it's all gone, and I'll divide it up between the six of us."

Ayden swallowed hard. He didn't know why they were going to divvy up the money between the six of them when there were as many as eight in the room with them. There were still several waitstaff on tonight as well as the manager.

"You got something to say?" He asked what he'd been thinking. "Oh well, we take care of our own here." He pulled out a gun from the back of his apron and shot the waitress in the head. "You'll sell off her meat too. It's good tasting, waitress meat, huh?"

Ayden looked down at his half-eaten steak and felt his belly lurch. Standing up, he barely made it out of the building's side door before he started throwing up every bit of food that was on his stomach. Christ, he'd been eating here every night for the past few weeks.

Staggering to the woods, he shifted and took off at a dead run so that his wolf could puke, too. Like a fool, he'd been shifting after work and letting his other part have the leftover meat from his meal. He'd be lucky if either of them would be able to eat steak again after this.

As he lay in the grass to rest, he heard voices. It was the manager, Mike Hendershot, and the cook, Harden Gray, talking about him. It took him a few seconds to realize that they weren't looking for him to play ball but were there to kill him.

"I thought that he could be one of us. Did you see his face when he realized what he was eating? Christ, that will sustain me for the rest of my life." A bullet pinged off the tree just above his head, but Ayden didn't move. "Well, Mikey, he's going to have to die now. You know that, don't you?"

"Yeah, it's a right shame. I was kinda liking him. Even though we do have to kill him off, do you think that I could have a taste of him? Damn, but I've never seen a nicer body than that man has. He must lift cars to keep in that good of shape. Can you imagine, Hardy, how muscled his butt rump would be to the person who would buy his roast?"

Ayden was going to be sick again, but he laid as still and quietly as he could. He could almost see them now. They were within five feet of him, leaning against the tree and talking. When one of them took a piss, he turned away from the man and reached out to his brother.

"I have a situation here that is going to make anyone sick that has ever eaten in this place I've been

working." Lica asked him if he was having fun anyway. *"I'm serious, Lica. They're selling off the meat that's left over. Also, oh Christ, I can't say this without puking. They're killing off the staff and selling them too as roasts, and – they've talked about selling me as a pot roast."*

"Where are you? I've told Brandy she's going to call the police as soon as you tell me where you are." He told him that he was at Red Rose Blues. *"That's not far from here, is it?"*

"No, about three miles outside of Coshocton. It's not hard to find. It has a big fucking rose that is at least fifty feet in the sky." He told his brother everything that he'd been told about the meat, as well as their plans for him. *"They shot a woman when I asked about how they were diving up the money six-ways when there were about eight of us back there. Just pulled out a gun and shot her right in the head. I never dreamed that they'd be selling the meat and making a profit off of it and then secondly, using human flesh...I can't deal with this right now."*

"The police are on their way. Brandy said that they were coming in without lights or noise. Just so they don't hurry up and get rid of the body." Lica told him about his day. *"We signed off on the paperwork*

this afternoon."

Ayden really didn't give two shits about what he'd done today. But then he realized that he was distracting him. Not only did his wolf seem to feel better, but he did as well. The other two men were still standing there talking when he slid his body along the damp grass to see if he could get to the parking lot. He wanted away from all the shit going on right now. He told his brother what he was doing.

"You'll have to talk to them, you know that, don't you?" He said he wouldn't be able to speak to anyone if they shot him. *"Good point. Yeah, I think you're better off getting away. But don't go back in – "*

"They're dragging out four bodies wrapped up in dark trash bags. I believe that they killed the other waitstaff before coming to find me." Lica said that Brandy wanted to hear so could he pull her into the conversation. *"I don't mind, but I'm going to tell you straight up that I'm not going to sugarcoat this."*

"I would expect no less from you. Are you all right, Ayden? Had I any idea what was going on, I'd never have sent you there. I'm so profoundly sorry that you had to witness this." Ayden told her that he'd do it again if she needed him to. He loved her like a

sister. *"And I love you all as my brothers. What's going on now?"*

"I'm following three men to a building I never noticed before. Do you know what it might be?" She told him that she didn't know there was a building. *"I'm assuming that...yes, I'm right, it's their slaughterhouse of sorts. Christ, there is so much blood all over the place that it's a small wonder that...Brandy, they have this down to a science. They're getting ready to saw cut the waitress shot they killed first. How do I get the police back here?"*

He ran to the parking lot, only taking time to look around for the cook and manager. As soon as he found one of the officers, who was a wolf, he bit gently into his hand so that they could speak. After telling him now through their link what was going on, he led him and two men back to the building.

Ayden was keeping his brother and sister updated on what was going on. The officer, Officer Merrick, said that he'd keep it out of the press and paperwork about how he had led them to the barn structure. But he would have to talk to them as a man. There was no way he'd be able to hide that he'd been in the building when things went south.

He wanted to ask him if he'd eaten there but

thought that was just too cruel. When it came out what some of the people might have been served, they were going to have about a million lawsuits on their hands. Ayden was glad that Brandy had only been thinking about investing in the expansion they wanted to have instead of owning it like he thought that she did.

It wasn't nearly as bad as he thought it might be. Ayden had expected there to be a gunfight, but almost as soon as the barn door was opened up, the four men that had brought the bodies down here dropped their equipment and surrendered. The first body had already been started on, and he had to leave before he got sick again.

The body, of course, had been removed from the kitchen. However, when he was shown the inside of the locker to hold the cold foods, he had to leave the place again. There was a woman hanging from a meat hook that had taken out her eye when her head was hooked in her skull.

"Everyone has been arrested. I'm currently hiding in the woods so that no one sees me. Officer Merrick said that they'd change his name and tell the public that he was one of the victims. It would be easy enough to hide from. They never got his name right in

the first place." Lica asked if he was coming home tonight. *"I think Merrick wants me to stick around and help them find the other body parts. They had to be doing something with their hands and feet."*

"Yes, I can see that. They'll need a great deal of help, I'm thinking." Lica then told him about how they'd found out that Brandy was a turned wolf. *"I had no idea, but I couldn't be happier. We've been looking it up. But Grannie seems to think that because I'm the alpha, Brandy will need to be a wolf as well."*

"Thank you both. I don't know what I would have done if either of you had freaked out with me. I know that I more than likely would have been shot." He looked out in the parking lot to see that the coroner was there. *"Wait, a second and a third have pulled into the lot too. If you want to know the names on the side, for now, all I can read is Forensic Van. I guess it could be from anywhere."*

Merrick had given him clothing when he had time to pull them from his trunk. He'd not realized how old the man was until he saw him with the light of the trunk. Ayden thought for sure that he would have been retired by now but didn't comment. The man was keeping everyone from freaking out, and that helped a great deal.

It was nearly midnight when he saw his brother and Brandy. The others, including his brothers, had come along to help search for the bodies if they needed them. Merrick said that they were all young pups so that they'd have a better chance of finding, as their 'sniffer' would be younger, too. As each one of them began to head for the woods, he still stayed where he was. He was afraid of messing up the plan that they had of him dying by a gunshot wound when the two men had chased him out of the restaurant. He was helpful by telling Merrick and the Feds, who had finally shown up where the bodies were. His family had been given bright green flags to put where the scent was that they'd found.

By the time the sun was coming up, they'd found sixty spots where the scent of blood was. In the first shallow grave, they found four sets of human appendages. Ayden thought that they'd find twice that many the longer his family was out there sniffing around. Brandy had made arrangements for food and water, as well as light food for the men working. Coffee was a huge seller, he noticed. Then Brandy came to sit on one of the few chairs and talked to him.

"I'm going to have to be more careful with people from now on." He didn't say anything because he was sure there was more to come. "I can't handle this shit anymore. I'd just like to stay at home, pound your brother, and, when the time comes, play with our baby. I'm seriously thinking of closing down this part of my business."

"What will you do with all that free time on your hands? Besides pounding my brother — which, by the way, is way too much information." She laughed like he hoped that she would. "I don't blame you one bit."

"A few weeks ago, a friend of mine was working at a bakery. He was, like you're doing, looking to see what was happening in the warehouse where things were sent from. Not only were the employees smoking and in the kitchen barefooted? But the place was so infested with rats — rats, not mice that when the bulldozer tried to take down one of the buildings, rats swarmed the man and his crew by going up the dozer and running after them." He told her to never tell him the name of the bakery. "I won't. Lica said the same thing when we were driving here. You'll be happy to know that I've never seen any of the product in any of your homes."

"Thank goodness for that." They both laughed that time. It relieved so much stress about this place. "I wanted to ask you something. I was wondering if you could give me a reference so that I could get a car loan. Doing this is wonderful, but I'm going to need a part-time job to make ends meet." She turned and looked at him.

"You should be getting paid?" Ayden told her that he didn't need to be paid so long— "No, I'm serious, you should be getting paid all along. I'd never expect anyone to be working for me that isn't going to get paid. That's not...I'll look into what's happened in the morning. All this time, I thought...Do you think that your brothers aren't being paid either? Christ, when I think about how many billable hours I'm going to owe Devlin if he's not being paid either. I might have to keep my doors open just to pay him off."

"He'd not want you to do that, Brandy. I hope you know that." She laughed, telling him that she'd been kidding. "Good. That kind of scared me a little bit."

By the time they were all headed home, over two hundred shallow graves had been found. A great many of them only had one person's parts in the grave, but a lot of them had more than three sets. It was enough to give him nightmares for the rest of his life.

Climbing into his bed, he was going to use some of his money. He hoped it was enough to get him a new mattress. Maybe some new towels. He laughed when he thought of some of the towels that his family used when living at home. The first towel that he ever had with nap and was thick was when he moved in with the Wilkins family when his mother had been arrested. He was going to get him some special things that he had picked out. He didn't care if they were new or antiques. Ayden wanted a home that was his and his alone.

"If only I'm going to be making enough money."

Before You Go...

HELP AN AUTHOR

write a review

THANK YOU!

Share your voice and help guide other readers to these wonderful books. Even if it's only a line or two, your reviews help readers discover the author's books so they can continue creating stories that you'll love. Log in to your favorite retailer and leave a review. Thank you.

AWARD WINNING, BESTSELLING AUTHOR

Kathi Barton, a winner of the Pinnacle Book Achievement Award and a best-selling author on Amazon and All Romance books, lives in Nashport, Ohio, with her husband, Paul. When not creating new worlds and romance, Kathi and her husband enjoy camping and going to auctions. She can also be seen at county fairs with her husband, an artist and potter.

Her muse, a cross between Jimmy Stewart and Hugh Jackman, brings her stories to life for her readers in a way that has them coming back time and again for more. Her favorite genre is paranormal romance, with a great deal of spice. You can visit Kathi online and drop her an email if you'd like. She loves hearing from her fans. aaronskiss@gmail.com.

Follow Kathi on her blog: http://kathisbartonauthor.blogspot.com/

www.ingramcontent.com/pod-product-compliance
Lightning Source LLC
Chambersburg PA
CBHW032004170626
46807CB00006B/2633